Hostile Horizon

Michael Ferguson

Published by Michael Ferguson, 2024.

This is a work of fiction. Similarities to real people, places, or events are entirely coincidental.

HOSTILE HORIZON

First edition. September 12, 2024.

Copyright © 2024 Michael Ferguson.

ISBN: 979-8227298973

Written by Michael Ferguson.

Table of Contents

Chapter 1: The Crash

The blaring sirens pierced through the roar of the engines as Flight 719 plummeted toward the ground. Inside the cabin, screams echoed like a symphony of terror, and the once-comfortable seats of the commercial flight became chaotic fragments in a world gone mad. The plane was falling fast, too fast, and no one on board could have known what awaited them below.

Alex Bishop, a marketing executive traveling for a conference, gripped the armrest with white knuckles as the plane shook violently. The overhead bins exploded open, spewing luggage across the cabin like missiles, and oxygen masks dangled uselessly above passengers. His pulse raced as he glanced at the faces around him—some twisted in silent prayers, others frozen in shock. The chaos of the moment seemed to stretch into eternity. Time itself felt warped.

And then, the impact.

The deafening sound of metal scraping against earth overwhelmed the senses as the plane crashed onto the unforgiving island terrain. Alex's body lurched forward as his seatbelt snapped tight against his chest, yanking him back like a ragdoll. The screeching of the fuselage grinding against trees and rocks was accompanied by the terrifying crackle of fire. Outside the windows, the world was a blur of flames and smoke, flashes of tropical greenery, and the looming presence of death.

For a moment, everything was silent—an eerie stillness filled the air, the calm after the violent descent. Alex's mind struggled to piece together what had happened. He coughed, the thick smoke invading his lungs, and forced his eyes open. His vision was blurred, and the coppery taste of blood filled his mouth. Shaking his head, he released the seatbelt with trembling hands, wincing at the pain that shot through his chest. His seat had somehow stayed intact, but the rest of the cabin was unrecognizable—twisted metal, debris, and bodies strewn about in haphazard positions.

"We're alive," Alex whispered to himself, his voice hoarse, as if the words themselves were a mantra against the horror he had just witnessed.

Around him, the groaning of the injured began to rise, a cacophony of pain and confusion. He stumbled forward, instinctively searching for any other survivors. The acrid stench of burning fuel filled the air, mixing with the tropical heat. The plane had broken into multiple sections upon impact, with debris scattered across the dense forest floor. It was a miracle anyone had survived.

"Help... someone, please..." A weak voice to his left caught Alex's attention.

He stumbled toward the sound, his legs unsteady beneath him. A young woman, no older than her mid-twenties, lay trapped beneath a metal beam, her face contorted in pain. Blood matted her hair, and her hands were trembling as she tried to free herself. Alex knelt beside her, the smoke stinging his eyes.

"I've got you," he rasped, though his own strength was wavering.

With a grunt, Alex heaved the beam off her leg, his muscles straining against the weight. As it clanged to the ground, the woman gasped in relief, tears streaming down her dirt-smeared cheeks. He helped her sit up, her breaths coming in ragged gulps.

"I thought... I thought I was going to die," she whispered.

"You're not alone," Alex said, though he wasn't sure how long any of them would survive. He scanned the area. More survivors were beginning to stir, their cries echoing through the wreckage.

A figure stumbled toward them—a man, tall and broad, dressed in a gray shirt torn at the shoulder. His face was bloodied, but his eyes were sharp. He looked like a soldier—disciplined, composed even amid the carnage. His gaze swept over Alex and the woman.

"Is she hurt?" the man asked, his voice steady despite the situation.

"Her leg's pinned, but I think she can walk," Alex replied, helping the woman to her feet. "We need to find more survivors and figure out where the hell we are."

The man nodded grimly. "I'm Max. We need to gather the others and get away from the plane. If this thing goes up, we don't want to be anywhere near it."

As Max moved to check on other survivors, Alex felt a strange sense of reassurance. Even in this nightmare, someone seemed to have their head on straight.

More survivors were crawling out from the twisted remains of the plane—injured, disoriented, but alive. Alex spotted an older man limping through the smoke, his face bruised, but determined. There was a mother holding a toddler, her eyes wide with fear, yet clutching her child as though she could shield him from the horror around them. Others, dazed and bleeding, wandered aimlessly, their minds not yet processing what had happened.

Within the hour, a ragged group of survivors had gathered near the edge of the crash site, away from the looming threat of the smoldering wreckage. Max had taken charge, his military background apparent in the way he assessed the situation.

"We need to move quickly," Max announced, addressing the group. "This fire could spread, and we don't know what kind of wildlife is out there. First priority is to get everyone accounted for and find shelter."

A murmur of agreement rippled through the crowd, though the fear in their eyes was palpable. They were trapped on a strange island, cut off from the world, with no way to call for help. The dense jungle loomed around them, its shadows seeming to shift with unseen movement.

Max organized search teams, and Alex found himself teamed up with a woman named Elena, the same woman he had rescued earlier. Together, they combed through the wreckage, calling out for any remaining survivors. The devastation was worse up close—bodies, some beyond recognition, lay still among the debris. The stench of death hung heavy in the air.

"Over here!" Elena shouted, pointing to a section of the plane's fuselage that had been torn open.

Inside, they found a man pinned beneath a row of seats, barely conscious. His breathing was shallow, and his skin pale.

Alex and Elena worked together to free him, dragging his limp form out of the wreckage.

"He's alive, but barely," Elena said, checking his pulse.

"We'll take him back to the others. Max said there's a clearing up ahead where we can set up camp."

By the time the sun began to sink below the horizon, casting long shadows over the island, the survivors had managed to gather what supplies they could from the wreckage—bottles of water, scattered food packets, a few first-aid kits. They had found a dozen survivors in total, though more were unaccounted for, lost in the jungle or buried beneath the wreckage.

The first night on the island was a blur of exhaustion and fear. The survivors huddled together in the makeshift camp, their faces lit by the flickering glow of a small fire. The tropical air was thick with humidity, and the jungle beyond the clearing buzzed with the sounds of nocturnal creatures.

But there was something else—a sound just on the edge of hearing, like the hum of machinery.

"Did you hear that?" Elena whispered, her eyes wide as she stared into the darkness.

Alex listened, his skin crawling. The sound was faint, but unmistakable—the whirring of something mechanical, something that didn't belong in the middle of the jungle.

Max stood up, his face grim. "Stay here," he ordered, his eyes scanning the trees. "I'll check it out."

As Max disappeared into the shadows, the remaining survivors exchanged nervous glances. The night seemed to press in around them, suffocating and oppressive. Alex's mind raced with questions. What had caused the crash? And what was that sound?

Minutes felt like hours as they waited for Max to return. Every rustle in the bushes, every flicker of movement, set their nerves on edge.

Finally, Max reappeared, his expression unreadable. He held something in his hand—something small and metallic.

"I found this in the trees," he said, holding it up to the firelight.

It was a drone.

The sun dipped below the horizon, casting long shadows over the wreckage of Flight 719. As the orange and pink hues of the sunset faded, the island was enveloped in an eerie twilight, and the thick jungle loomed like a dark, impenetrable wall. The survivors, battered and bruised, huddled around makeshift fires. For the first time since the crash, silence fell over them, but it was not the comforting kind. It was the type of silence that weighed heavy in the air, thick with unease and fear of the unknown.

Max, a man of few words but commanding presence, walked between the groups, checking on the injured. His military training had kicked in shortly after the crash, taking charge as the chaos of the impact subsided. Now, with nightfall creeping in, he was even more on edge. His instincts told him this island was not the paradise it appeared to be.

"How's everyone holding up?" he asked Sarah, a nurse who had been tending to the wounded.

Sarah looked up from her makeshift medical station, where she was stitching up a gash on a young man's leg. Her face was streaked with dirt and sweat, but her hands remained steady.

"They'll survive for now," she said, her voice strained. "But we need proper supplies. I can't do much with what we have."

Max nodded. They had managed to salvage some items from the wreckage—water bottles, a few first-aid kits, and some food rations—but it wasn't nearly enough for the long haul. The jungle surrounding them was dense and foreboding, and Max had already sent out a small group earlier to scout for more resources. They hadn't returned yet.

"Let me know if anything changes," Max said, before moving on.

He passed by smaller groups of survivors—families, lone travelers, and the few flight attendants who had made it through. Their faces were a mix of shock and disbelief, still trying to process the nightmare they had woken up to. The murmurs of conversation died down as he walked by, everyone watching him with a mixture of hope and fear. Max knew what they were thinking: What now?

Just as he was about to check in with another group, a sharp voice broke the silence.

"Look!" someone shouted. "Up there!"

Max whipped his head around to see a man pointing towards the sky. At first, he saw nothing, just the deepening twilight and the faint outline of stars beginning to twinkle. But then, a glimmer caught his eye—a metallic glint moving through the sky.

A drone.

It hovered silently above the treetops, its red light blinking in the darkness.

"That's not one of ours, is it?" Sarah asked, standing up from her patient.

Max frowned. "No, it's not."

The drone hovered for a moment longer, then slowly began to drift away, disappearing into the jungle's shadows.

The group was silent, the sight of the drone chilling them to the bone. The presence of technology—so precise, so deliberate—felt out of place in the wildness of the island. It wasn't just a sign of civilization, but of someone watching them.

"We need to get inside the plane, or what's left of it," Max said suddenly, his voice urgent. "Everyone, grab what you can and head back to the fuselage. We'll use it as shelter tonight."

The survivors scrambled to follow his orders, grabbing whatever scraps of supplies they had gathered during the day. Some clutched onto seat cushions or bits of metal from the wreckage, anything that could serve as a makeshift weapon, just in case.

As they moved toward the remains of the plane, the darkness seemed to close in around them. The jungle, which had been a green maze of leaves and vines during the day, now felt like a living thing, breathing and pulsating with hidden threats.

Max led the way, his sharp eyes scanning the treeline for any movement. He had been trained to sense danger long before it revealed itself, and right now, every fiber of his being was on high alert.

Once inside the fuselage, the survivors set up camp as best they could. The shell of the plane offered little protection from the elements, but it was better than being exposed out in the open. Fires flickered in the darkness, casting long, dancing shadows against the curved walls of the wreckage.

"We need to keep watch tonight," Max said, addressing the group. "I'll take first shift. We'll rotate every few hours."

He didn't have to explain why. The drone had said enough.

As Max settled into his watch position near one of the plane's gaping windows, his mind raced with questions. Who was operating the drone? And why? Were they here to help, or were they something more sinister?

Hours passed, and the night deepened. The jungle was alive with the sounds of unseen creatures—chirps, rustles, and the occasional guttural growl that echoed from deep within the trees. Every noise set Max's nerves on edge, but he remained focused, scanning the perimeter for any signs of movement.

Suddenly, there was a sound—a faint metallic clink coming from somewhere nearby.

Max tensed, his hand instinctively reaching for the metal pipe he had fashioned into a weapon earlier. He stood slowly, straining his ears to catch the direction of the sound. It was coming from the jungle, just beyond the treeline.

He motioned for Sarah, who was sitting nearby, to stay quiet as he stepped out of the fuselage and into the night.

The moon had risen, casting a pale, silvery light over the island. Max moved cautiously, his every step deliberate and silent. The metallic sound came again, louder this time, like metal scraping against metal.

He reached the edge of the treeline and paused, peering into the darkness.

There, in the distance, he saw it—a shape, large and looming, partially hidden by the thick foliage. It looked like a structure, something man-made. A bunker?

Max's heart raced. He took a step closer, careful not to make a sound. But before he could get a better look, the sound of footsteps behind him made him freeze.

He turned sharply, his weapon raised, only to find Sarah standing there, wide-eyed and holding a flashlight.

"Max," she whispered, her voice trembling. "Did you hear that?"

Max nodded, his eyes darting back to the strange structure in the distance. "We need to get back to the others. Now."

They made their way back to the fuselage in silence, the weight of the discovery pressing heavily on their minds. As they approached, Max could see the others still huddled around their fires, oblivious to what lay just beyond the treeline.

"We're not alone here," Max said quietly to Sarah as they reentered the wreckage. "And whatever's out there, it's not friendly."

The night dragged on, filled with tension and the constant hum of the jungle. Every now and then, the survivors would hear the faint whir of a drone passing overhead, its red light blinking ominously in the distance.

By the time dawn began to break, the survivors were exhausted, both physically and mentally. But Max knew that the real challenges were only just beginning. The island held secrets—dark, dangerous secrets—and they were about to uncover them.

As the first rays of sunlight pierced through the trees, Max stood up and addressed the group.

"Today, we search the island. We need to know what we're dealing with."

The others nodded, their faces grim but determined. They had survived the first night, but the worst was yet to come.

Chapter 2: Survival Instincts

The sun had barely begun to rise when Max stirred from his restless sleep, his body aching from the crash and the hard ground he'd slept on. Around him, the other survivors lay scattered, some still unconscious, others slowly coming to life as the early morning light filtered through the thick canopy of the jungle. A few had already begun to gather themselves, inspecting the wreckage for anything useful, while others sat in stunned silence, their minds still grappling with the enormity of what had happened.

Max stood, stretching his sore limbs, and surveyed the scene. The remnants of Flight 719 were strewn across the beach and into the jungle beyond. Metal twisted into unnatural shapes, seats ripped from their frames, and scattered luggage marked the path of destruction that had been carved out by their crash landing. It was a miracle anyone had survived at all.

But survival was only the beginning.

He'd been in situations like this before, although none quite as dire. His time in the military had prepared him for disaster scenarios, but this felt different. There was something unsettling about this island, something that gnawed at the back of his mind, even as he tried to focus on the task at hand.

They needed structure. They needed leadership.

Max had spent years as a soldier, leading men into combat, making decisions that meant life or death for those around him. He could see the same need for leadership here. These people were lost, scared, and without direction. If they didn't get organized quickly, panic would set in, and that was the last thing they needed.

He strode toward a group gathered near the edge of the jungle, where a few of the more able-bodied survivors were rummaging through the wreckage, searching for anything that could be of use. Water, food, medical supplies—anything that could help them survive the next few days.

"Everyone, listen up!" Max's voice rang out, cutting through the murmur of quiet conversation. The group turned to face him, eyes wide and expectant. "We need to get organized. This isn't a vacation. We're stranded, and we don't know how long we're going to be here. First priority is making sure everyone's accounted for and safe. Then we can figure out a plan."

A few of them nodded in agreement, relief flickering in their eyes. They needed direction, and Max was more than willing to give it.

"We need teams," Max continued. "One group to gather supplies, another to find fresh water, and another to start setting up a camp. We can't just sit around waiting for rescue."

"I'll help with supplies," a tall, muscular man volunteered. His clothes were torn, and his face was smeared with dirt, but his posture was steady. Max recognized the type immediately—someone used to hard work, probably construction or something similar.

"What's your name?" Max asked.

"Josh," the man replied, offering a grim smile. "I've done some survival training. I'll help where I can."

"Good," Max said. "You're in charge of gathering supplies. Take whoever you need."

Josh nodded, already scanning the crowd for able-bodied volunteers.

A woman stepped forward next. She was shorter, with a determined expression and a first-aid kit clutched in her hand. Her dark hair was pulled back in a loose ponytail, and despite the dirt and exhaustion etched across her face, there was a calmness in her eyes that Max found reassuring.

"I'm a nurse," she said. "I've already started treating some of the injured, but we're going to need more supplies if we're going to keep everyone alive."

Max nodded. "What's your name?"

"Claire," she replied. "I'll handle the medical side of things, but I need help."

"I'll assist her," another woman chimed in. "I've got some basic first aid training." She looked younger, maybe in her twenties, with wide eyes that betrayed her fear, but there was a determination in her voice that Max respected.

"Good," Max said, mentally noting their roles. "We need fresh water and shelter, too. Anyone who's up for a scouting mission, come with me. The rest of you, start clearing a space for camp."

For a moment, no one moved, and Max could feel the weight of their hesitation. These people weren't soldiers; they weren't used to hardship or making life-or-death decisions. They were ordinary civilians, thrown into a nightmare. But if they were going to survive, they needed to trust him.

Finally, a few people stepped forward, willing to follow his lead. Max nodded and began organizing them into groups, delegating tasks as efficiently as possible.

He was about to head into the jungle with the scouting party when a voice cut through the air behind him.

"Who made you the boss?"

Max turned to see a man approaching. He was younger, mid-thirties maybe, with slicked-back hair and an air of arrogance that rubbed Max the wrong way immediately. His clothes were clean, his posture almost too relaxed for the situation they were in.

"I'm just trying to get us organized," Max replied evenly, not wanting to escalate the situation. "We don't have time to sit around waiting. We need a plan."

The man scoffed. "And you think you know better than the rest of us?"

Max could feel the eyes of the group shifting between the two of them, tension hanging in the air. He took a deep breath, keeping his tone measured. "I have experience in situations like this. We need to work together if we're going to survive."

The man folded his arms across his chest, a smirk playing on his lips. "Maybe we don't want a dictator running the show. Maybe we should vote on who's in charge."

Max stared at him, his jaw clenching. This was the last thing they needed right now—division and conflict. But he also knew that forcing his authority wouldn't help. He needed to defuse the situation, not escalate it.

"Look," Max said, stepping forward. "This isn't about power. It's about survival. I'm not trying to be in charge—I'm just trying to keep us alive. If someone else has a better plan, I'm all ears."

For a moment, the man seemed taken aback, his smirk faltering. He glanced around, as if expecting support, but the rest of the group remained silent, their eyes fixed on Max.

"Fine," the man said after a tense pause, his voice laced with sarcasm. "You want to play hero? Go ahead. But don't expect everyone to follow your lead."

With that, he turned and walked away, leaving Max standing there, frustration bubbling beneath the surface. He knew this wouldn't be the last challenge to his authority. In any group, especially one under this kind of stress, there would always be dissenters. But he couldn't let it distract him. There were more important things to focus on.

"Alright," Max said, turning back to the group. "Let's get moving. Time's not on our side."

As the small scouting party followed him into the jungle, Max's mind was already racing with thoughts of how they would survive the coming days. Food, water, shelter—all critical to their immediate survival. But beyond that, something else gnawed at him. The strange sounds they'd heard the night before, the unsettling presence he'd felt watching them—it wasn't just paranoia.

Something was wrong with this island.

They pushed through the dense foliage, the air thick with humidity, insects buzzing around them as they made their way deeper into the jungle. The farther they went from the crash site, the more isolated and eerie the surroundings became. The jungle was alive with sounds—the rustle of leaves, the calls of distant birds, the occasional snap of a branch—but beneath it all, there was a strange, almost mechanical hum that seemed to come from everywhere and nowhere at once.

"What do you think that is?" one of the survivors asked, his voice shaky.

Max paused, listening. The hum was faint but persistent, like the distant whir of machinery buried deep beneath the earth. It didn't fit with the natural sounds of the jungle, and it set Max's nerves on edge.

"I don't know," Max admitted, scanning the dense trees for any sign of danger. "But we're not alone here."

The group exchanged uneasy glances, fear creeping into their expressions.

"Let's keep moving," Max said, his tone firm. "We need to find water and a safe place to set up camp."

They continued through the jungle, the oppressive heat and thick vegetation making every step feel like a battle. Hours passed, and just when Max was beginning to worry that they wouldn't find anything useful, one of the scouts called out.

"Over here!"

Max pushed through the underbrush to where the scout was standing, and his heart leapt when he saw it: a small stream, the water clear and cool as it trickled over rocks.

"Fresh water," Max said, relief washing over him. "This is what we needed."

The group gathered around the stream, filling their hands with water and drinking greedily. For a moment, the weight of their situation lifted, replaced by the simple relief of having found something that could keep them alive.

But the relief was short-lived.

Max's eyes caught something on the far side of the stream—a glint of metal, barely visible through the thick foliage. He frowned, stepping closer to get a better look.

"What is it?" one of the scouts asked, noticing his hesitation.

Max didn't answer right away. He moved closer, brushing aside the leaves and vines that obscured his view. What he saw sent a chill down his spine.

It was a hatch—metal, rusted at the edges, but unmistakably man-made. It was partially buried in the ground, hidden by years of overgrowth, but there was no mistaking what it was.

A door.

Max stared at it, his mind racing. This island was supposed to be uninhabited. They were in the middle of nowhere, far from any known civilization. And yet here it was, undeniable proof that someone—or something—had been here before them.

"What the hell is this place?"

The air was thick with humidity as Max and Ethan trudged through the jungle, their feet sinking into the damp soil. The dense foliage around them buzzed with the sounds of insects and the occasional rustle of something unseen in the undergrowth. But what drew their attention now was the door. Max knelt beside it, brushing away years of accumulated dirt and leaves, revealing more of its metallic surface.

"It's definitely a bunker," Max said, his voice low and cautious.

Ethan stood behind him, his face pale, as he stared at the mysterious door. "What do you think is inside?"

Max ran his hand over the cold, smooth surface of the door, looking for a handle or lever. "I don't know," he said. "But I think it's something important. There's no way this thing was built here by accident."

Ethan's breath was unsteady as he nodded, his eyes fixed on the structure. Max found a small panel on the side of the door, half-covered by rust. He pressed his fingers against it, hoping it might reveal some way to open the entrance. After a few moments of searching, his fingers caught on a latch hidden beneath the grime.

"Got it," Max whispered, gripping the latch and pulling hard.

With a grinding sound that echoed through the jungle, the door creaked open, releasing a faint gust of stale air. The passage beyond was shrouded in darkness, but as Max's eyes adjusted, he could see a faint glow emanating from somewhere deep within. It was dim, almost like the flicker of dying lights, but it was unmistakably artificial.

Ethan stepped forward hesitantly, peering into the bunker. "We shouldn't go in there."

Max glanced over his shoulder at Ethan. "You want to survive, don't you? We need to know what's going on here. This bunker could have answers."

Ethan swallowed hard but nodded. Max took a deep breath and stepped into the darkness, his boots echoing against the metallic floor of the bunker. The air inside was cool, almost unnaturally so, as if it hadn't been disturbed in years. The passageway descended steeply, and Max could hear the faint hum of electricity in the walls, a sign that the bunker still had power, at least partially.

They walked in silence, their footsteps heavy in the enclosed space. Max kept his hand against the wall to steady himself as the floor sloped downward. The dim glow grew stronger as they moved deeper into the bunker. After a few more steps, they reached a larger chamber, and the source of the light became clear.

In the center of the room stood several monitors, flickering with static. A faint hum filled the air, and a low, mechanical beeping echoed from the walls. Max approached the nearest monitor, squinting at the screen. It was showing what looked like live footage, but the signal was distorted. He tapped the side of the monitor, and the image cleared for a brief moment.

"What the hell?" Ethan whispered, standing beside him.

The monitor displayed an overhead view of the island, captured by what appeared to be a drone. Max could see the coastline, the jungle, and their camp in the distance. But there was something else—something that made his blood run cold. Several red dots were moving across the screen, their paths marked with precise, calculated movements. The dots were converging on the camp.

"Are those people?" Ethan asked, his voice shaking.

Max's jaw clenched. "No. Those are drones, like the one we saw last night. They're tracking us."

Ethan stared at the screen in horror. "They know where we are. They're watching everything we do."

Max nodded grimly. "And they're closing in."

His mind raced as he scanned the room. The monitors weren't the only thing in the bunker. Along the far wall, rows of metal crates were stacked neatly, each one marked with military insignia. Max walked over to one and pried it open with a grunt. Inside, he found weapons—high-tech rifles, sidearms, and grenades, all in pristine condition.

"Jesus," Ethan muttered, staring at the weapons. "This isn't just some abandoned bunker. This is a military stockpile."

Max picked up one of the rifles, examining it closely. "Not just any military," he said. "Look at this tech. These weapons are more advanced than anything I've seen in the field."

Ethan paced nervously, his eyes darting between the weapons and the monitors. "What does this mean? Who put this here?"

Max's mind churned with possibilities. The island, the drones, the weapons—it was all connected to something much larger than a simple crash. This bunker was part of a military operation, one that had been planned and executed with precision. But why? And who was behind it?

"We need to get back to camp," Max said, slinging the rifle over his shoulder. "We need to tell the others."

Ethan hesitated, glancing at the monitors again. "What if they're already there? The drones, I mean. What if it's too late?"

Max gripped his shoulder. "Then we fight. But we have to warn them, no matter what."

With that, they turned and made their way back up the narrow passage. The bunker's oppressive darkness seemed to close in on them as they climbed, and the faint hum of electricity grew quieter with each step. By the time they reached the surface, the sun was beginning to set, casting long shadows across the jungle.

Max scanned the horizon, his eyes sharp. "Let's move. We don't have much time."

They sprinted through the jungle, weaving between trees and leaping over fallen branches. Max's heart pounded in his chest as the weight of the rifle pulled at his back. He could feel the tension rising in his gut, a primal instinct telling him that danger was closing in. They had to reach the camp before the drones did.

As they approached the clearing where the survivors had set up camp, Max slowed to a stop, raising a hand to signal Ethan. They crouched behind a thick grove of trees, scanning the area. The camp was quiet, too quiet. The usual sounds of conversation and movement were absent, replaced by an eerie stillness.

"Something's wrong," Ethan whispered.

Max nodded, his eyes narrowing. "Stay close."

They crept forward, moving silently through the underbrush. When they reached the edge of the camp, Max's worst fears were confirmed. The tents were overturned, supplies scattered across the ground. There was no sign of the other survivors, but the camp had clearly been ransacked.

"What happened here?" Ethan asked, his voice barely audible.

Max's gaze swept over the scene, his mind working quickly. "The drones. They must've attacked while we were gone."

Ethan swallowed hard, his eyes wide with fear. "Where is everyone?"

Max didn't have an answer. The camp was abandoned, and there were no obvious signs of a struggle. But the overturned tents and scattered supplies told him that whatever had happened, it had been fast and violent. He scanned the treeline, his senses on high alert.

"They might still be out there," Max said, his voice low and tense. "We need to find them before it's too late."

Ethan nodded, clutching a knife he had picked up from the ground. "Lead the way."

Max moved cautiously through the camp, his rifle at the ready. His eyes flicked between the trees and the sky, watching for any sign of movement. The air was thick with tension, and every rustle of the leaves set his nerves on edge.

Then, from somewhere deeper in the jungle, Max heard it—a faint, metallic buzzing. It was the sound of a drone.

"They're coming," he hissed.

Ethan's face went pale. "What do we do?"

Max's mind raced. They couldn't stay in the open, not with the drones closing in. But they couldn't run blindly into the jungle either. They needed to find the other survivors and regroup before making their next move.

"We need to find higher ground," Max said. "We'll have a better chance of spotting the drones and figuring out where the others went."

Ethan nodded, his grip on the knife tightening. Together, they slipped back into the jungle, moving swiftly but quietly. Max led the way, his eyes scanning the terrain for anything that could give them an advantage. The sound of the drone grew louder as they climbed a nearby hill, the trees thinning out around them.

At the top of the hill, Max crouched behind a boulder, pulling Ethan down beside him. From their vantage point, they could see most of the camp below. Max's breath caught in his throat as he spotted them—four drones, hovering silently over the clearing, their red lights scanning the ground.

"They're looking for something," Ethan whispered.

Max nodded, his eyes locked on the drones. "They're looking for us."

Ethan swallowed hard. "What do we do now?"

Max didn't answer immediately. His mind was already working on a plan. They couldn't take on the drones directly, not with just the two of them. But they had the element of surprise, and they had the weapons from the bunker. If they could disable even one of the drones, they might have a chance to figure out who—or what—was controlling them.

"We take them down," Max said finally, his voice steady. "One by one."

He handed Ethan one of the rifles from the bunker. "Stay low, and aim for the sensors. We need to disable them before they spot us."

Ethan nodded, though Max could see the fear in his eyes. They didn't have time to waste. The drones were circling the camp, their red lights casting an eerie glow over the jungle. Max took a deep breath, steadying his nerves.

"On my signal," he whispered.

He raised his rifle, lining up the first shot.

Chapter 3: Tensions Build

Max's heart raced as he scanned the jungle from their precarious vantage point. The four drones hovered ominously over the camp, their red lights sweeping across the clearing like sentinels. He could feel the pressure mounting, every instinct telling him that time was running out.

Ethan crouched beside him, his breath coming in shallow, anxious bursts. "What do we do now?"

Max didn't answer immediately. His eyes were fixed on the drones, their movements methodical and calculating. They were searching for something, and Max had a sinking feeling that their search was not just random surveillance but part of a more sinister agenda.

"We need to move," Max said finally. "We can't stay here with those things overhead. They'll spot us if we stay out in the open."

Ethan nodded, his face pale but resolute. "Where do we go?"

Max considered their options. The jungle offered dense cover but was also full of its own dangers. The safest route might be to move to higher ground, where they could better assess the situation and potentially find the other survivors. He glanced around, searching for a path that would lead them away from the immediate danger.

"Follow me," Max said, rising cautiously. He led Ethan down the hill and into the thicker part of the jungle, where the undergrowth was even denser. They moved silently, every snap of a twig feeling like a gunshot in the oppressive quiet.

As they made their way through the jungle, Max's mind raced with theories about what was happening. The drones, the abandoned camp—it all pointed to something far more complex than just a plane crash. There had to be a reason for all this, and Max was determined to uncover it.

They reached a small clearing and paused to catch their breath. Max checked his surroundings, his eyes darting from tree to tree. The sound of the drones was faint now, but Max knew they could be closing in again. He took out a map he had found in one of the bunkers and spread it on the ground.

"Based on the layout of the camp and the terrain, we should head towards this area," Max said, pointing to a spot on the map. "It's higher ground, and it's away from the main camp. We might find a better vantage point or even some sign of the other survivors."

Ethan nodded, his eyes scanning the map. "And if we don't find anyone?"

Max's jaw tightened. "Then we focus on figuring out what's really going on here. We need to understand the situation before we can make any decisions."

They resumed their journey, moving with renewed purpose. The jungle grew denser as they climbed, the air thick with humidity and the smell of decay. Max's senses were on high alert, every rustle and snap making him more wary. The jungle was alive with sound, but Max was focused on their objective.

Hours passed, and the sun began to set, casting long shadows across the landscape. The temperature dropped slightly, but the oppressive humidity remained. Max and Ethan found a small, sheltered area where they could rest and regroup.

Max pulled out the encrypted files they had found in the bunker and began examining them again. The documents were filled with technical jargon and military codes, but Max had a feeling they contained important information. He had managed to decrypt a few sections earlier, revealing bits about surveillance and tracking, but the full scope of the project remained a mystery.

Ethan sat nearby, sharpening a knife he had found in the wreckage. His hands trembled slightly, and Max could see the fear in his eyes. The sight of the drones and the abandoned camp had clearly taken a toll on him.

"Do you think the others are still alive?" Ethan asked, his voice barely above a whisper.

Max looked up from the documents, meeting Ethan's gaze. "I hope so. But we have to be prepared for the possibility that something happened to them. We can't afford to be optimistic or to let our guard down."

Ethan nodded, though he looked unconvinced. "What do you think the drones are looking for? Are they tracking us?"

Max leaned back against a tree, his mind racing through possibilities. "I think they're part of a larger operation. They could be monitoring us for a reason—maybe to see how we react to stress, or to gather data on our survival skills. Whatever it is, it's not just about keeping us from escaping."

Ethan's face was drawn with worry. "So what do we do if we find the others? Do we tell them everything?"

Max hesitated. "We need to be careful. If there's a chance that some of them might be part of this experiment, we have to keep our plans close to our chest. We don't know who we can trust."

The thought of potential betrayal weighed heavily on Max's mind. He had already seen the seeds of discord among the survivors, and the disappearance of one of their own would only exacerbate the situation. Trust was a fragile commodity in their current circumstances, and Max knew that maintaining unity would be crucial to their survival.

The night fell swiftly, and the jungle grew darker around them. Max and Ethan settled into their makeshift shelter, trying to get some rest despite the mounting tension. Max's thoughts were filled with images of the drones and the abandoned camp. He could not shake the feeling that something much more sinister was at play.

In the dead of night, Max was jolted awake by a sudden, sharp sound. He sat up quickly, his heart pounding. Ethan was already awake, his eyes wide with fear.

"What's happening?" Ethan whispered.

Max listened intently, trying to pinpoint the source of the noise. There was a faint, rhythmic thumping coming from the direction they had just come from—a sound that seemed out of place in the natural ambiance of the jungle.

"I don't know," Max said, rising cautiously. "But we need to check it out."

They moved silently towards the source of the sound, their senses heightened. The thumping grew louder as they approached, and Max could see a faint glow through the trees. It was as if something was emitting a steady, pulsating light.

As they reached the edge of the clearing, Max's breath caught in his throat. In the center of the clearing was a large, metallic structure, partially obscured by foliage. It was a massive, cylindrical object, its surface covered with strange symbols and patterns. The pulsating light seemed to emanate from within the structure.

"What is that?" Ethan asked, his voice trembling.

Max didn't have an answer. The object was unlike anything he had ever seen, and its presence here was deeply unsettling. He approached cautiously, his mind racing with possibilities. The structure could be part of the island's surveillance system, or it could be something else entirely—something that was integral to the experiment.

As they got closer, Max noticed a small door on the side of the structure, slightly ajar. The pulsating light was stronger now, casting eerie shadows across the ground. Max exchanged a look with Ethan, then carefully approached the door.

Inside, the structure was dimly lit by a series of flickering lights. The interior was filled with complex machinery and equipment, some of which seemed to be malfunctioning. Max's eyes were drawn to a large screen mounted on one wall, its display showing a series of graphs and charts.

Max approached the screen and studied it closely. The graphs were filled with fluctuating lines and numbers, but there was one thing that stood out—a series of red dots moving across a map of the island. The dots seemed to represent different locations, and their movements were tracked in real-time.

Ethan peered over Max's shoulder, his eyes widening as he took in the sight. "What does it mean?"

Max shook his head. "I'm not sure. But it looks like we're being monitored. These dots might be tracking our movements or the movements of the drones."

The realization hit Max like a cold wave. The island was a controlled environment, and they were being watched every step of the way. The structure was part of a larger system designed to observe and analyze their behavior.

"We need to get out of here," Max said, his voice low and urgent. "If they're monitoring us, they might already know we're here."

Ethan nodded, and they quickly retraced their steps, moving back towards their shelter. The weight of their discovery pressed heavily on Max's shoulders. The island was no longer just a survival challenge—it was a stage for a sinister experiment, and they were the unwilling participants.

Back at their shelter, Max tried to piece together everything he had learned. The drones, the mysterious structures, the surveillance system—it all pointed to a carefully orchestrated operation designed to test their limits. But who was behind it, and why?

He looked over at Ethan, who was staring into the darkness with a haunted expression. The fear in his eyes was palpable, and Max knew that the situation was more dangerous than ever. Trust was already in short supply, and now there was the added burden of knowing that they were being watched.

"We have to stay focused," Max said, trying to offer some reassurance. "We need to find the others and figure out what's really going on here."

Ethan nodded, though his expression remained grim. "How do we even begin to figure out something this complex?"

Max sighed, feeling the weight of responsibility bearing down on him. "One step at a time. We start by finding the others and making sure they're safe. Then we gather more information and try to make sense of it. We have to stay one step ahead of whatever or whoever is controlling this place."

As they settled back into their shelter, the jungle around them seemed to close in with an oppressive sense of unease. The unseen forces at play were far more dangerous than they had initially imagined, and the challenge of survival had taken on a new, more terrifying dimension. Max knew that they were only at the beginning of a much darker journey, and the road ahead was fraught with peril.

The night stretched on, filled with the sounds of the jungle and the persistent hum of the drones overhead. Max and Ethan lay awake, their minds racing with the possibilities and dangers that lay ahead. The island was no longer a simple challenge of survival—it was a battlefield of psychological warfare, and the true test of their strength and resolve had only just begun.

The evening was descending upon the island, cloaking the jungle in a dense, unsettling darkness. The survivors had gathered around the makeshift camp, their faces etched with worry. The atmosphere was thick with unspoken fears and the oppressive weight of uncertainty. Max and Ethan had barely managed to secure their shelter when they noticed that something was terribly amiss. The supplies they had painstakingly gathered and rationed seemed to be dwindling at an alarming rate.

Max's suspicion had been piqued when he noticed that the food supplies, particularly the dried meat and canned goods, appeared to be lower than they should have been. What was once a controlled inventory now seemed to be running out far too quickly. It wasn't just the dwindling supplies that worried him; it was the feeling that something was systematically going wrong.

"I can't believe this," Max muttered, examining the empty food containers. "We've only been here a few days, and we're running out of food faster than we should."

Ethan, who had been organizing their makeshift kitchen area, glanced up with concern. "You think someone's taking it?"

"It's possible," Max replied, his mind racing. "We need to be sure. If we're being watched, they could be tampering with our supplies to drive us to desperation."

Max's growing paranoia was beginning to infect the rest of the group. Whispers and glances had turned into accusations and confrontations. Without concrete proof, it was difficult to point fingers, but trust was quickly eroding.

That night, as the group huddled around a small fire, the tension was palpable. Accusations were made in hushed tones, and the air was thick with suspicion. Max tried to maintain order, but his authority was being increasingly challenged. Some of the survivors, frustrated by the lack of progress and the mounting paranoia, began to question his leadership.

"We can't keep going on like this," Alex, a civilian who had been vocal in his dissatisfaction, said. "We need to find out who's sabotaging our supplies before it's too late."

Max's patience was wearing thin. "I'm doing everything I can to keep us safe. We don't have the luxury of time to play detective."

The conversation was cut short by a sudden commotion near the edge of the camp. A loud crash, followed by hurried footsteps, shattered the uneasy silence. The survivors scrambled to their feet, grabbing whatever makeshift weapons they had managed to scavenge.

Max and a few others rushed toward the source of the noise, their hearts pounding in their chests. They found a group of people gathered around a fallen crate. The crate, once full of food, was now lying on its side, its contents scattered across the ground.

"It's been tampered with!" one of the survivors shouted. "Someone's been going through our stuff!"

Max took a deep breath, trying to control his rising frustration. "Everyone, calm down. Let's take a closer look."

As Max examined the scene, he noticed something odd. The crate had been deliberately knocked over, and the food inside had been spread out in a way that suggested it wasn't just a random accident. The deliberate nature of the tampering made it clear that someone was trying to create chaos.

"It's not just about stealing food," Max said, addressing the group. "This is a deliberate attempt to drive us apart. We need to find out who's behind it."

The accusations continued to fly, each person pointing fingers at someone else. The atmosphere in the camp was growing more hostile by the minute. The fear of being sabotaged was beginning to overshadow the need to work together for survival.

As the night wore on, Max and Ethan decided to investigate further. They retraced their steps, examining the area around the camp for any signs of intrusion. They found nothing conclusive, but the sense of unease persisted.

Meanwhile, inside the bunker, a different kind of tension was building. The encrypted files that Max had discovered were proving difficult to decipher, but they contained enough disturbing information to raise further concerns. The documents hinted at psychological manipulation experiments, suggesting that the survivors were not only being watched but were part of a larger, more sinister agenda.

Max and Ethan returned to the camp with their findings. The decrypted sections revealed a series of experimental protocols designed to induce stress and conflict among participants. The realization that their situation might be part of a controlled experiment added a new layer of dread to their already precarious existence.

"We need to be careful," Max warned the group as they gathered around the fire. "There's a chance that the sabotage is part of a larger plan to manipulate us. We need to stay united, or we're playing right into their hands."

The survivors listened, but the fear and suspicion had already taken root. The once-unified group was now fracturing under the strain of their circumstances. Each person was grappling with their own fears and doubts, and the sense of solidarity that had initially brought them together was beginning to crumble.

In the days that followed, the sabotage continued. Food supplies mysteriously vanished, and personal belongings were tampered with. Trust was a scarce commodity, and every interaction was laced with suspicion. The once-cohesive group was now a collection of individuals, each with their own agenda and fears.

Max found himself increasingly isolated. His attempts to maintain order and unity were met with resistance from those who felt he was overstepping his authority. The tension between Max and Alex, who had been vocal in his criticism, reached a boiling point.

"Look, I get that you're trying to keep us together," Alex said one night as the two of them faced off near the campfire. "But your approach isn't working. We need to address the real issues, not just keep everyone in line."

Max's patience was wearing thin. "I'm trying to keep us alive, Alex. If you have a better idea, let's hear it."

Alex's frustration was evident. "We need to find out who's behind this. If we don't, we're just going to tear each other apart."

Max and Alex's argument was interrupted by another commotion near the camp. The survivors gathered, their faces etched with concern. A small fire had broken out near one of the tents, threatening to spread to the rest of the camp.

The fire was quickly extinguished, but the damage had already been done. The survivors were once again thrown into chaos, their resources further depleted. Max's attempts to regain control were met with increasing resistance, and the fractures within the group were becoming more pronounced.

As the days turned into weeks, the survivors' situation grew increasingly dire. The constant sabotage and internal strife left them exhausted and on edge. The psychological strain was taking its toll, and the once-clear lines of authority and trust were becoming blurred.

Max knew that they needed to find a way to address the underlying issues if they were going to have any hope of surviving. The encrypted files from the bunker offered some clues, but deciphering them was proving to be a slow and arduous process.

The situation came to a head when another survivor went missing. The group had been on edge for days, and the disappearance was the final straw. Accusations flew, and tensions reached a boiling point. The group was on the brink of collapse, and Max knew that something had to change.

In a desperate bid to regain control, Max called a meeting. The survivors gathered, their faces a mix of fear and anger. Max addressed them, his voice steady but filled with urgency.

"We need to stop this," Max said, his gaze sweeping over the assembled group. "The sabotage and the accusations are tearing us apart. We need to focus on surviving and finding a way off this island. We can't afford to let ourselves be divided."

The survivors listened, their expressions reflecting a mix of skepticism and hope. The sense of unity that Max was trying to reestablish was fragile, but it was their only chance.

Max knew that the road ahead would be difficult. The challenges they faced were not just physical but psychological, and the strain of their situation was beginning to show. The island was no longer just a hostile environment; it was a battleground of the mind, and the stakes were higher than ever.

As the survivors reluctantly agreed to put aside their differences, Max hoped that they could find a way to work together. The island's true nature was still a mystery, and the danger they faced was far from over. But for now, the immediate threat of internal conflict had been temporarily addressed, and Max was determined to use this fragile truce to uncover the truth behind their situation.

In the coming days, the survivors would face new challenges and revelations. The island's secrets were slowly being revealed, and the psychological manipulation that had been at work was beginning to take its toll. The struggle for survival was far from over, and Max knew that the path ahead would be fraught with danger and uncertainty.

The night was long, and the jungle around them was filled with the sounds of unseen creatures and the occasional distant hum of the drones. Max lay awake, his mind

Chapter 4: Deadly Discoveries

The tension in the camp was palpable as the survivors gathered around the fire, their faces illuminated by the flickering light. The recent sabotage of their food supplies had left them on edge, and accusations had begun to fly. Max, trying to maintain control, faced the brunt of the anger. His leadership had been questioned from the beginning, but now, with their basic needs compromised, the dissenters grew bolder.

Lena, one of the survivors who had found the bunker in the previous days, stood up, her face grim. "We need to figure out who did this. We can't just sit here and hope it stops."

Max nodded in agreement. "We need to stay united. We can't let this divide us further."

A murmur of agreement went through the group, but there was an undercurrent of distrust. They had already been through so much, and now this betrayal added a new layer of complexity to their situation. The sabotage had not only affected their morale but had also jeopardized their chances of survival. With their food supplies tampered with, their options were limited. They had already begun rationing their remaining food, and the prospect of an extended stay on the island without adequate supplies was grim.

As the group discussed their next steps, Max's mind raced. He had hoped that the bunker they had discovered would provide some answers, but so far, it had only deepened the mystery. The encrypted files they had found hinted at something much larger than just their immediate predicament. Psychological manipulation experiments, covert military operations—these were not the kinds of things they could easily brush aside.

The survivors split into smaller groups to search for clues and to discuss strategies. Max took Lena, Sarah, and Dave aside to talk privately. They gathered in a secluded area of the camp, away from the prying eyes of the others.

"I think we need to do a thorough search of the camp," Max said, his voice low. "We need to find out who might be behind this."

Lena looked worried. "But who could it be? We've all been together since the crash. How could someone sabotage us without anyone noticing?"

Dave shook his head. "It could be someone who has been biding their time. We've seen drones and heard strange noises. It's possible someone has been working with these forces."

Max's gaze was steely. "We need to check the perimeter of the camp and see if there are any signs of tampering. If we can find out how they got to the food, we might be able to figure out who did it."

The group dispersed, each member of the search party taking a different direction. As they scoured the camp and its surroundings, they discovered several unusual things. Footprints near the food storage area were not their own, and some of the containers had been tampered with. It became clear that someone had deliberately manipulated their supplies.

Hours passed, and the sun began to set. The survivors reconvened at the campfire, their faces tired and tense. Max addressed the group, his voice firm.

"We've found evidence that someone here is working against us. The footprints and the tampered containers suggest that we have a traitor among us."

The announcement was met with a wave of murmurs and uneasy glances. Suspicion fell on everyone, and the unity they had managed to build began to crumble further. Accusations were hurled, and voices were raised. Max tried to restore order, but it was clear that trust had been severely damaged.

In the midst of the chaos, Sarah, a young woman who had been quiet for most of the day, stepped forward. "I found something strange near the perimeter," she said, her voice trembling. "There were signs of movement—like someone had been hiding there."

Max turned to her. "What kind of movement?"

"Footprints, broken branches. It looked like someone had been trying to stay hidden," Sarah explained.

Max's mind raced. If someone had been hiding and observing them, it could mean they were being watched even when they thought they were safe. The realization added a new layer of fear to their already dire situation.

"We need to investigate this area more thoroughly," Max said. "Tonight, we'll form teams to watch the perimeter. We need to catch whoever is behind this before they do more damage."

The survivors reluctantly agreed, and the night was filled with the sounds of shifting footsteps and whispered conversations as they took turns on watch. The tension was high, and sleep was elusive for many.

As the hours dragged on, the darkness seemed to close in on them. The jungle was alive with sounds, some familiar and some disconcertingly alien. Every snap of a twig or rustle of leaves was met with heightened alertness. The fear of an unseen enemy grew stronger with each passing hour.

By dawn, the survivors were exhausted, but they had not spotted anyone suspicious. The food supplies had been thoroughly examined, and it was clear that the sabotage had been executed with precision. Someone knew exactly what they were doing and had access to their supplies.

Max called a meeting to discuss their next steps. The group gathered, weary but resolute. Max addressed them with a mixture of urgency and determination.

"We've been sabotaged, and we need to find out who is responsible. It's clear that our situation is more dire than we thought. We need to remain vigilant and work together to uncover the truth."

The survivors nodded, their expressions a mix of fear and determination. They knew that their survival depended on finding the traitor and understanding the full scope of the threats they faced.

As the day wore on, Max continued to pore over the encrypted files they had found in the bunker. He hoped that they might provide some insight into the nature of the experiment they were part of. The files hinted at psychological manipulation and advanced technology, but their full meaning remained elusive.

Max knew that the only way to truly understand their predicament was to confront the forces manipulating them. The drones, the mysterious noises, and the unexplained sabotage were all part of a larger puzzle. As he reviewed the documents, he became increasingly convinced that their survival depended on uncovering the truth about the island and its hidden agendas.

Meanwhile, the tension among the survivors continued to build. Accusations and mistrust simmered beneath the surface, threatening to erupt into open conflict. The sabotage had not only jeopardized their immediate needs but had also fractured their fragile sense of unity.

Max and his team worked tirelessly to uncover clues and gather information. They conducted thorough searches of the camp and its surroundings, hoping to find any additional evidence of the sabotage. The sense of urgency was palpable, and each new discovery only added to the complexity of their situation.

The group remained on high alert, their nerves frayed by the constant threat of an unseen enemy. The knowledge that someone among them was working against them only heightened their sense of paranoia and mistrust. As the days passed, it became increasingly clear that their situation was far more dangerous than they had initially realized.

In the face of mounting challenges and growing tension, the survivors had to decide whether to unite against the external threats or allow their internal divisions to tear them apart. The struggle for survival had taken on a new dimension, and the stakes had never been higher.

The survivors had scarcely settled back into their camp after the grim discovery of their deceased companion. The shock and grief were still fresh, and the camp's atmosphere was thick with fear and suspicion. That evening, as the survivors attempted to regroup and make sense of the day's horrors, they were confronted with a new and unsettling reality.

Max, who had been trying to maintain order amidst the chaos, called for a meeting at the central fire. His voice carried the weight of authority, but even he couldn't mask the anxiety etched into his face. The survivors gathered around, their faces illuminated by the flickering firelight, casting shadows that seemed to dance with their fears.

"I know everyone's shaken up right now," Max began, "but we need to focus. There's a lot we don't understand, and we need to figure out our next steps."

The group nodded, though their eyes betrayed a mix of exhaustion and apprehension. Among them were Lena, the sharp-witted journalist who had been documenting their experiences, and Greg, a retired engineer who had proven useful in scavenging the island's hidden resources.

"I found something earlier today," Greg said, his voice trembling slightly. "While we were exploring the island, I stumbled upon another bunker. This one was different from the others."

Max raised an eyebrow. "Different how?"

"It was deeper underground," Greg explained. "And it had more advanced technology. I think it's connected to what we found earlier. The bunker had a bunch of files and equipment that looked like it was meant for some high-level research."

Lena's eyes widened. "Research? What kind of research?"

"I don't know for sure," Greg admitted. "But the files were marked with something called 'Project Horizon.' I couldn't understand much, but it seems like the project involves advanced technology and psychological manipulation."

Max's expression grew serious. "If this is true, then everything we've been experiencing might be part of some grand experiment. We need to see these files for ourselves."

As the group moved to the makeshift command center—a collection of tarps and crates serving as their headquarters—Greg carefully laid out the files and pieces of equipment he had retrieved. The documents were encrypted, their contents indecipherable without the proper codes. The technology, on the other hand, was a mix of familiar and alien: devices that resembled both military gear and high-tech surveillance tools.

Lena picked up a small, sleek device with a glass interface. "This looks like a data storage unit. Maybe it holds information that could give us more insight into what's really happening here."

Greg nodded. "It could be. We need to find a way to access the data."

The group's attention was suddenly diverted by a rustling noise coming from the edge of the camp. Everyone tensed, their eyes darting toward the sound. Max motioned for silence, and the group fell still, straining to hear any further noises.

"What was that?" Lena whispered.

"I don't know," Max replied, his voice low. "But we should be on alert."

The tension was palpable as the survivors waited, their nerves frayed by the day's events. After a few moments, the noise ceased, and Max signaled for the group to resume their tasks. They continued examining the files and equipment, trying to piece together the puzzle.

As night fell, the survivors took turns standing guard, their eyes scanning the darkness for any signs of movement. The fire crackled softly, providing a meager source of warmth and light in the cold night air.

Lena sat by the fire, poring over one of the encrypted documents. "This one mentions something about psychological stress tests. It looks like they've been monitoring our responses to various stimuli."

"Does it say anything about how we can get out of here?" Max asked, his voice tinged with frustration.

"Not directly," Lena replied. "But there's a reference to 'Subject Withdrawal Protocols.' It might be related to how they manage or control us."

Greg, who was working on another piece of equipment, looked up. "We need to figure out how to use this tech to our advantage. If we can access the data or disable some of their systems, we might find a way out."

The group continued their work late into the night, their minds racing with possibilities and theories. The discovery of the additional bunker and its contents had opened up new avenues of investigation, but it also raised more questions about the true nature of their predicament.

As the hours passed, the survivors began to feel the weight of exhaustion settling in. The physical and mental strain of the day's events was taking its toll, and the once-cohesive group was starting to show signs of strain and division.

Max, feeling the burden of leadership, called a brief halt to their activities. "We need to rest. We've made progress, but we can't afford to burn out. We'll resume our work in the morning."

The group reluctantly agreed, and they settled down for the night, their minds heavy with the uncertainty of their situation. The survivors huddled in their makeshift shelters, their sleep restless and filled with unsettling dreams.

In the darkness, the island seemed to close in around them. The dense jungle whispered with unseen voices, and the occasional crackle of a hidden drone reminded them that they were never truly alone. The campfire's dying embers cast long, eerie shadows, adding to the sense of unease.

As dawn approached, the survivors awoke to a new day filled with the promise of more challenges and discoveries. They were determined to uncover the truth about Project Horizon and find a way to escape the island, but the increasing complexity of their situation made the task seem increasingly daunting.

The hidden agendas of their captors and the advanced technology at their disposal only added to the growing sense of desperation and confusion. The survivors knew that their time on the island was running out, and they needed to act quickly to uncover the full extent of the experiment and secure their escape.

With renewed determination, the group set out to continue their investigation, their eyes open for any further clues that might lead them to freedom. They were no longer just survivors of a crash; they were participants in a high-stakes experiment, fighting against forces they barely understood.

Chapter 5: Fractured Trust

The sun was barely peeking over the horizon when the survivors gathered at the camp, the chilling aftermath of the previous day's events still hanging heavily in the air. Max, who had been trying to maintain some semblance of order, now faced a growing rebellion. Alex, a civilian survivor with an unexpectedly sharp mind, had been vocal about his dissatisfaction with Max's leadership. His grumbling had transformed into a full-blown challenge.

The camp was a mess. The makeshift tents and shelters, hastily assembled in the wake of the crash, were now in disarray. A few survivors were engaged in quiet conversations, their eyes darting around nervously as if expecting another attack at any moment. Max's stern face was etched with fatigue as he addressed the group.

"We need to focus on finding a way off this island. We can't keep going in circles," Max said, his voice carrying a tone of authority that had previously been respected. But today, the respect was strained.

Alex, a tall man with a commanding presence despite his civilian status, stepped forward. "And how exactly are we supposed to do that, Max? We don't even know what's really going on here. You keep telling us to follow your lead, but so far, it's led us nowhere."

Max's eyes narrowed. "I'm doing the best I can with the information we have. What's your plan, Alex? You've been quick to criticize but slow to offer solutions."

Alex's eyes hardened as he glanced at the others, who were now watching the exchange with growing interest. "I think we need to question everything. How do we know we can trust you? You've been in charge from the start, and now we're losing people."

A murmur of agreement rippled through the group. Max's leadership, which had once seemed unassailable, was now under scrutiny. His sense of urgency had been interpreted by some as a lack of transparency.

"We're all in this together," Max said, trying to keep his voice steady. "We need to work as a team. I understand there are doubts, but now isn't the time for division."

But Alex wasn't finished. "That's the problem. We're supposed to trust each other, but how can we when we're kept in the dark? I think we need to reassess our situation and consider if there's someone else who might have a better plan."

The group fell silent. Alex's challenge had struck a nerve. The fear and frustration that had been simmering beneath the surface were now bubbling up, and the once-cohesive group was beginning to splinter into factions.

Max tried to regain control. "Listen, we need to focus on survival. Whether or not you agree with my leadership, we have to stick together if we want any chance of getting off this island."

"Maybe sticking together isn't enough," Alex countered. "Maybe we need to look at our situation from a different angle. I've been thinking—what if the drones and the bunkers are part of a bigger game? Maybe there's more to this place than just a hostile environment."

Max frowned. "What are you suggesting?"

"I'm suggesting that we might be part of an experiment," Alex said. "The drones, the bunkers, everything—it doesn't add up. We need to find out what's really happening here."

Max's face grew darker. "And how do you propose we do that? We've already found bunkers with advanced technology. What else do you think we need?"

Alex shrugged. "We need to gather more information. We need to understand who's behind all this. If we can find the source of these operations, we might be able to turn the tables."

Max hesitated. He knew Alex's points had merit, but he was reluctant to let his authority be undermined. "Fine. We'll investigate further. But we have to be careful. We don't know what we're dealing with."

With that, the group reluctantly agreed to split into factions. One faction, led by Max, would continue searching for ways to escape and secure their immediate surroundings. The other, led by Alex, would focus on investigating the island's mysteries, hoping to uncover more about the strange occurrences and the nature of their predicament.

The division was palpable. Max's faction consisted mostly of those who valued order and discipline, including a few former military personnel and pragmatic survivors. Alex's faction included those who were disillusioned with the current situation and were eager to explore new possibilities, including some who had been more skeptical of Max's leadership.

The factions set off in different directions. Max led his group deeper into the jungle, focusing on securing resources and establishing a more defensible position. They worked with a sense of urgency, knowing that their survival depended on their ability to adapt and respond to new threats.

Meanwhile, Alex's faction began exploring the island's perimeter, searching for any clues that could shed light on their situation. They were cautious but determined, driven by a growing sense that there was something sinister behind the island's mysteries.

As the day wore on, the two factions worked tirelessly. Max's group cleared debris, set up better defenses, and scouted for additional resources. They found a fresh water source and managed to establish a more secure perimeter around their new camp.

Alex's group, on the other hand, stumbled upon a series of strange markings on trees and rocks. The symbols seemed to be part of a code or language, and their discovery only deepened the mystery of the island. The markings led them to another hidden bunker, this one even more advanced than the previous ones they had found. It was filled with data storage units, surveillance equipment, and more encrypted files.

By evening, the tensions between the factions had grown. Max and Alex's groups had become increasingly isolated from each other, and the lack of communication only fueled suspicion and mistrust.

Back at Max's camp, the mood was tense. The group had successfully fortified their position and gathered supplies, but there was an underlying unease. The feeling of being watched persisted, and the survivors couldn't shake the sense that they were being monitored from the shadows.

Alex's faction, having made some progress in deciphering the symbols and exploring the new bunker, was more optimistic. They had uncovered more information about the island's infrastructure and were beginning to piece together a picture of what might be happening.

As night fell, the two camps settled into uneasy routines. Max's group gathered around a fire, discussing their plans and trying to stay vigilant. The night was quiet, but the survivors remained on edge, knowing that their situation was far from stable.

Alex's group, meanwhile, huddled around their new findings. The bunker's encrypted files revealed more about the island's surveillance capabilities and hinted at a broader network of control. They were hopeful that the information they had uncovered would lead them to answers, but they knew that time was running out.

In the darkness, the island seemed to hold its breath. The survivors were caught in a delicate balance between hope and despair, trust and suspicion. As they prepared for another night in their fractured world, the true nature of their predicament remained shrouded in uncertainty.

The division between the factions was now a critical factor in their survival. Max and Alex were at odds, each leading their respective groups with a different vision of how to navigate the island's dangers. The stakes were high, and the survivors knew that their ability to work together—or their failure to do so—could determine their ultimate fate.

As the night wore on, the island seemed to pulse with hidden threats. The survivors were caught in a web of intrigue and danger, and the coming days would test their resolve and their ability to trust—or betray—each other.

The chaos was immediate and intense. The survivors, scattered by the sudden attack, struggled to make sense of the disorienting, tear-filled cloud enveloping their makeshift camp. It wasn't just the gas—the screams, shouts, and the distant whir of drones made it feel like they were under siege.

Max, already in a vulnerable state from his earlier injuries, was knocked off his feet by a blast of tear gas. His vision blurred, and he stumbled through the thick, choking smoke, trying to call out for his team. The camp was disintegrating around him; tents were torn, supplies scattered, and the faint outlines of panicked survivors darted in every direction.

In the midst of the turmoil, Alex and his faction saw their opportunity. The rift between them and Max's group had widened significantly. They saw the attack as a chance to seize control. As Max tried to orient himself, he could hear the muffled voices of Alex's faction urging others to follow them, promising safety away from the chaos.

"Stay with me!" Max shouted through the smoke, but his voice was swallowed by the cacophony of panic. He could barely see through his stinging eyes, the gas making it nearly impossible to breathe. He stumbled toward the edge of the camp, where he knew the few remaining members of his group were trying to regroup.

The air was thick with the acrid scent of chemicals. Max groped for his radio, his fingers finding it amid the wreckage. He tried to call for help, but static and unintelligible voices were all he received in response. His team's voices were lost in the chaos, and he could only hope they were trying to make their way to safety.

Through the smoke, he saw figures darting past him—some were carrying supplies, others dragging injured comrades. The desperation in their movements was palpable. Max forced himself to focus, moving with determined, albeit shaky, steps towards what he hoped was the direction of his remaining team members.

In the dense smoke, visibility was almost non-existent. Max's breathing was labored, and every inhale brought a burning sensation to his lungs. He pushed through, his senses overwhelmed by the disorienting effects of the gas. His goal was to find a secure location where they could regroup and plan their next move.

As he stumbled through the smoke, he caught glimpses of Alex's group setting up their own camp on the far side of the clearing. It was a strategic move—by abandoning the area, Alex's faction was positioning themselves as the new leaders. Max could see the makeshift barricades and shelters being erected hastily.

Max finally reached a semi-sheltered spot behind some large rocks, where a few of his team members had also found refuge. They were disoriented but managed to stay together, huddled and trying to catch their breath. Max joined them, leaning against a boulder and trying to shake off the effects of the gas.

"We need to get out of here," Max said hoarsely, his voice cracking. "Alex's group is making their move."

One of his team members, a former medic named Sarah, was tending to another survivor who had collapsed. She looked up, her face a mask of determination. "We need to regroup and figure out our next step. We can't stay here. It's too dangerous."

Max nodded, his mind racing. The attack had shifted the dynamics of the group drastically. Alex's faction, having seized the opportunity, was now in a position to challenge Max's authority. The camp was in ruins, and their supplies were likely compromised.

"Let's move to the northern side of the island," Max suggested. "It's less exposed, and we might find some cover there."

With their decision made, the survivors began to gather what little they could salvage from the wreckage. The chaos had left them disorganized, but they knew they had to act quickly. Every minute they spent in the open was a minute they risked further attacks.

Max and his team carefully made their way towards the northern part of the island, moving through the dense jungle. The path was rough, with low-hanging branches and tangled underbrush, but it provided some cover from the drones that might still be hovering above.

As they walked, Max could feel the tension among his group. The attack had not only made their situation more precarious but had also deepened the divisions within their ranks. Alex's faction was growing more assertive, and the remaining survivors were uncertain of whom to trust.

In the relative safety of the northern jungle, Max's team began to set up a new temporary camp. They worked quickly, using what supplies they had salvaged to create makeshift shelters and start a fire. The smoke from the fire was a small comfort, offering warmth and a semblance of normalcy amidst the chaos.

"We need to get a handle on this situation," Max said as he surveyed their new camp. "Alex's group is likely planning their next move. We can't let them gain the upper hand."

Sarah, now taking on a leadership role within the group, nodded in agreement. "We should also consider that the drones are still a threat. We need to find a way to either disable them or at least stay off their radar."

Max agreed. The drones had proven to be a significant threat, and their ability to track and attack without warning made them a constant danger. They needed to come up with a plan to either evade or neutralize them.

As night began to fall, the survivors settled into their new camp. The dark jungle around them felt oppressive, the sounds of the island's wildlife blending with the distant hum of drones. The group was exhausted, both physically and mentally, and the tension between the factions was palpable.

Max took a moment to reflect on the situation. The attack had been a wake-up call, highlighting the fragility of their current situation. They were not just stranded—they were in a deadly game with unknown rules, and every decision could mean the difference between life and death.

In the dim light of the fire, Max gathered his core team members for a strategy meeting. Sarah, a few others who had managed to stay with Max, and a couple of new faces who had joined them after the chaos were present. The mood was somber but focused.

"We need to secure this position and start gathering intelligence on Alex's group," Max began. "We also need to figure out the best way to deal with the drones. Any ideas?"

One of the new members, a tech-savvy young man named Jason, spoke up. "I've been trying to work out a way to hack into the drone's frequency. If we can gain control of them, we might be able to use them to our advantage or at least disable them."

Max's eyes lit up with cautious optimism. "That could be our best bet. But it's risky. We need to be careful not to draw too much attention to ourselves."

Jason nodded. "I understand. I'll work on setting up a makeshift signal jammer to see if we can block the drones' communications. It might not be perfect, but it's a start."

As the meeting concluded, Max felt a renewed sense of determination. The survivors were facing unprecedented challenges, but they had to remain focused. The island was no longer just a place of survival; it had become a battleground of control and deception.

The night wore on, with the survivors working in shifts to maintain their defenses and keep watch. The new camp was a small but vital refuge in a situation that seemed to spiral further out of control with each passing day.

Max lay awake, listening to the sounds of the jungle and the distant whir of the drones. He knew that the fight for survival was far from over. The attack by the drones had changed the game, and now, more than ever, he had to be vigilant. The island was a hostile horizon, and only by navigating its dangers with strategy and resolve could they hope to escape its grasp.

The survivors faced a long and uncertain road ahead, but in the darkness of the jungle, they clung to the hope that they could turn the tide against their unseen enemies. The struggle for survival was no longer just a battle against nature—it was a fight against an insidious force that sought to manipulate and control them.

As the first light of dawn began to filter through the canopy, Max knew that the real challenge had only just begun. They had to regroup, adapt, and confront the threats that lay ahead, both within their ranks and beyond. The island was not just a test of endurance—it was a crucible where trust and betrayal would determine their fate.

Chapter 6: The Trap

The survivors had managed to regroup after the tear gas attack, but the temporary safety they found was short-lived. The remnants of their camp lay scattered, the scent of smoke mingling with the pervasive humidity of the island. They had scavenged what they could and were now huddled together in the relative safety of a dense grove of trees. The once-familiar jungle now seemed alien, every shadow concealing an unknown threat.

Max, his face smeared with soot and blood from the attack, scanned the perimeter with a wary gaze. His leg was bandaged hastily with a strip of his shirt, but the injury was a constant, throbbing reminder of their precarious situation. His eyes met those of the survivors around him, and he could see the same anxiety reflected back. The tension was palpable, their minds strained from the relentless pressure of their circumstances.

"Everyone needs to stay alert," Max said, his voice harsh but commanding. "We don't know if they'll come back or if they'll send something worse."

Anna, one of the few who had managed to stay calm, spoke up from where she sat against a tree trunk. "We need to figure out what's really going on here. The drones, the bunkers, the food sabotage—it's all too coordinated to be random."

The group fell silent, the only sounds the rustling of the leaves and distant, eerie calls of nocturnal animals. Their thoughts were interrupted by James, who had been studying the encrypted files they had recovered from the bunker. His face was drawn and pale under the dim light of their makeshift campfire.

"I've been trying to decrypt these files," James said, his voice wavering. "But I think I've found something. It's not just about survival. This island—there's something else at play."

Max turned sharply. "What do you mean? What have you found?"

James hesitated before continuing. "It looks like the island is part of an experiment. The files mention something called 'Project Horizon.' It's supposed to be a psychological manipulation experiment. They're trying to see how people react under extreme stress."

A murmur of disbelief swept through the group. For the first time, the notion that they were not merely stranded but part of a larger, sinister experiment began to sink in.

"You're saying this whole thing is a setup?" Claire, a young teacher among the survivors, asked. "That they're controlling everything we're experiencing?"

James nodded. "That's what it looks like. And it gets worse. There are references to advanced technologies used for psychological warfare, and it's clear that our perceptions are being manipulated."

A heavy silence settled over the group. The weight of their situation seemed to press down on them, more suffocating than the smoke and tear gas they had recently endured. It wasn't just the physical danger anymore; it was their very minds being used as battlegrounds.

"I think we're being watched," Max said, breaking the silence. "But it's not just the drones. There are other things—strange noises, feelings of déjà vu. I'm starting to wonder if they're trying to mess with our heads."

As if on cue, a sudden chill swept through the air, causing everyone to shiver involuntarily. The forest seemed to shift and breathe around them, the shadows growing longer and more menacing.

The survivors began to experience strange phenomena. Lila, who had been relatively quiet since the attack, suddenly clutched her head, her face contorted in pain. "Something's wrong," she said, her voice trembling. "I—I can't remember where I was before the crash."

A sense of dread spread through the group. Max and James exchanged worried glances. They had heard reports of disorientation and memory loss from the bunker files, but seeing it firsthand was different.

"Everyone, stay calm," Max urged. "Try to focus on what you know. We need to keep ourselves together if we're going to get out of this."

But the psychological assault was relentless. Survivors began to report strange hallucinations: vivid, disturbing images that seemed all too real. Some saw shadowy figures moving in the periphery of their vision, while others experienced flashbacks to events that hadn't happened.

Claire, who had been dozing off near the campfire, woke up with a start. Her face was pale, her eyes wide with terror. "I saw—" she began, but her words faltered. "I saw someone I knew. It was my brother, but it couldn't have been. He's—he's gone."

The group struggled to maintain their composure, but the growing sense of paranoia and fear was almost tangible. Trust eroded with each passing hour, as everyone began to question whether their memories were their own or something implanted by their unseen captors.

Max tried to take control of the situation, but the psychological warfare made it increasingly difficult. He could see the strain on everyone's faces, the fear and confusion making it harder to distinguish friend from foe. The line between reality and manipulation was blurring, and every interaction seemed tinged with suspicion.

The hallucinations grew more intense. James reported hearing whispers in the jungle, voices that seemed to come from nowhere and everywhere. Anna claimed to have seen a figure in the distance, but when she investigated, there was no one there.

By the second night after the attack, sleep was almost impossible. The survivors huddled together, their minds racing with fear and uncertainty. Each noise in the jungle became a potential threat, each shadow a possible predator.

Max decided to take a different approach. He gathered the group together and made a decision. "We need to explore the island further. We need to find more answers, and we need to see if there's a way to counter whatever they're doing to us."

The survivors, though apprehensive, agreed. They were desperate for answers, even if that meant facing the unknown dangers of the island.

As they set out, the forest seemed to close in on them. The trees, thick and foreboding, cast long, tangled shadows that played tricks on their already troubled minds. The survivors moved cautiously, their eyes scanning for any signs of the strange phenomena that had plagued them.

The journey through the jungle was grueling. The air was thick with humidity, making each step feel like wading through a dense fog. The trees seemed to whisper and moan, their leaves rustling with an unsettling rhythm. The survivors could feel the weight of the island pressing down on them, a constant reminder of their precarious situation.

As they ventured deeper, the forest grew quieter. The usual sounds of wildlife fell away, replaced by an eerie stillness. The survivors felt their anxiety mount with each passing moment. The lack of familiar sounds was unnerving, heightening their sense of vulnerability.

Hours later, they stumbled upon an old, overgrown path. It looked as if it had not been used in years. The path seemed to lead somewhere significant, and they decided to follow it in hopes of finding something that could explain the bizarre occurrences.

The path led them to a clearing, where a large, abandoned building stood. It was partially covered in vines and surrounded by dense foliage. The building had an ominous, imposing presence, its dark windows staring blankly at them.

Max led the way as they approached the structure. The building was made of concrete, with a heavy metal door that appeared to be rusted shut. The survivors gathered around it, their hearts pounding with a mix of hope and trepidation.

"This might be one of the bunkers we've heard about," Max said, his voice low. "Let's see if we can get inside."

The group worked together to pry open the door. It creaked and groaned as it swung open, revealing a dark interior.

The survivors hesitated, but Max took a deep breath and stepped inside. The others followed, their flashlights cutting through the darkness.

The interior of the building was dusty and filled with cobwebs. The air was stale, and the only sound was the echo of their footsteps on the concrete floor. They explored the building, searching for anything that might provide answers.

In one room, they found a series of monitors and control panels. The equipment was outdated but still operational. James approached the control panels, his fingers moving over the buttons and switches.

"This looks like a control room," James said, his voice tinged with excitement. "We might be able to find some useful information here."

As James worked to access the data, the survivors continued to search the building. They found more advanced technology, including surveillance equipment and communication devices. It became clear that this building was part of the island's network of facilities, designed to monitor and control their environment.

The survivors' discovery of the control room brought a mix of hope and dread. They had found evidence of the experiment's infrastructure, but the reality of their situation became even more unsettling. The island was not just a prison; it was a meticulously controlled environment designed to test their limits.

As James accessed the data, he found files that confirmed their fears. The files detailed various psychological experiments and the methods used to manipulate their perceptions. It became evident that the experiment was more complex and insidious than they had imagined.

"We need to use this information to our advantage," Max said, his voice resolute. "We need to understand their methods and find a way to fight back."

The survivors continued to gather information, their minds racing with the implications of their discoveries. The psychological warfare they were experiencing was no accident; it was a deliberate tactic designed to break them down.

As night fell, the survivors prepared to return to their temporary camp. The building's dark, oppressive atmosphere had taken its toll on them. The psychological strain was beginning to show, and they needed to regroup and plan their next move.

The journey back through the jungle was tense. The survivors were on high alert, their senses heightened by the fear and uncertainty that had become their constant companions. Each rustle in the underbrush and each distant sound was a potential threat.

When they finally reached their camp, they were exhausted and on edge. The discoveries they had made had provided some answers, but they had also deepened the mystery of their situation. The island was a sophisticated trap, designed to test their mental and emotional resilience.

As they settled in for the night, the survivors were left to grapple with the reality of their predicament. The psychological warfare they were facing was not just a series of random events; it was a carefully orchestrated plan designed to break their spirits.

Max sat alone by the fire, his mind racing with thoughts of their next move. The information they had uncovered was crucial, but it was only the beginning. They needed to remain vigilant and united if they were going to survive the experiment and find a way off the island.

The night was filled with strange sounds and unsettling visions. The survivors tried to rest, but sleep was elusive. The psychological manipulation was relentless, and the line between reality and illusion continued to blur.

As dawn approached, the survivors knew that they had to face whatever challenges lay ahead. The island was a hostile environment, both physically and mentally, and they had to find a way to fight back against the forces controlling their fate.

Their journey was far from over, and the true nature of the experiment was only beginning to unfold. The survivors were determined to uncover the truth and escape the island, but the psychological warfare they were facing was just the beginning of their ordeal.

The survivors' world had become a twisted maze of fear and confusion. The psychological manipulation they were subjected to was only growing more intense. Every decision felt like a gamble, and every moment was fraught with anxiety.

It was in this heightened state of paranoia that several members of the group were captured. Their disappearance was sudden and terrifying. One minute, they were part of the group, discussing the latest horrors they had faced; the next, they were gone. The others searched frantically for them, but the island seemed to have swallowed them whole.

Max, who was still nursing his injuries from the previous attack, was beside himself with worry. The loss of these survivors was a severe blow to their already fragile morale. He knew they needed answers, but finding the missing was becoming increasingly difficult.

The remaining survivors convened at the makeshift camp, trying to piece together any clue that might lead them to their friends. Among them, Max's second-in-command, a resourceful woman named Claire, took charge of organizing the search efforts. "We need to find them," she urged, her voice steady despite the fear in her eyes. "We can't afford to lose anyone else."

As they combed through the dense forest, they found evidence of a struggle—a torn piece of clothing, a dropped flashlight, and broken branches. It was clear that the captives had been dragged away. The survivors' fear was palpable, their faces etched with grim determination.

Meanwhile, the captives were being transported to an underground facility, hidden deep within the heart of the island. The facility was a stark contrast to the tropical landscape above. It was a cold, sterile environment, filled with the hum of machinery and the harsh glare of fluorescent lights. The captives, disoriented and frightened, were shoved into a large, dimly lit room.

The room was furnished with metal chairs and a single large table in the center. On one wall, there was a large screen displaying a live feed of the island above. The room was eerily quiet, save for the occasional buzz of the fluorescent lights.

The captives, including Anna, a mother of two who had been desperately trying to keep her children safe, and Ethan, a former paramedic, were shackled to their chairs. They exchanged worried glances, trying to assess their situation. The room's cold atmosphere was a harsh reminder of the inhumanity of their situation.

Anna tried to comfort her children, who were visibly shaken. "We'll be okay," she whispered, though her voice trembled. Ethan, who had been trying to stay calm and composed, scanned the room for any potential means of escape.

The door to the room creaked open, and a figure entered, clad in a white lab coat and a face mask. The figure was tall and imposing, and their voice was distorted by a speaker attached to the mask. "Welcome to our facility," the figure announced, their tone cold and devoid of empathy. "You are part of an experiment designed to test the limits of human endurance and psychological resilience."

The captives stared in shock as the figure continued, revealing the true nature of their predicament. "Your memories have been altered. The plane crash was staged. Everything you remember is a fabrication."

The revelation was met with gasps and cries of disbelief. Anna's face turned pale as she struggled to process the information. Ethan clenched his fists, his mind racing with thoughts of how they might escape.

The figure stepped closer, placing a small device on the table. "This is a memory stimulator," the figure explained. "It will allow us to monitor and manipulate your memories further. The experiment is far from over."

The captives' fear intensified as they realized the full extent of their situation. The figure's words were chilling, and the implications of their new reality were almost too much to bear.

As the figure left the room, the captives were left to grapple with their new reality. The memory stimulator was a constant reminder of the control the experimenters had over their lives. They were trapped in a nightmarish scenario where their memories and perceptions were being manipulated for someone's twisted pleasure.

Back at the survivors' camp, Max and Claire were strategizing their next move. They knew they had to rescue their friends, but the facility's location remained a mystery. They had only the scraps of information they had gathered to guide them.

Max's thoughts were consumed with the possibility that the facility might hold the key to their escape. "We need to find out where they're keeping our friends," he said, his voice filled with resolve. "There must be a way in."

Claire nodded, her expression determined. "We'll start by searching for any signs of the facility's location. We can't afford to waste time."

The search was exhaustive, with the survivors combing every inch of the island for any clues. They examined the terrain, looking for anything that might hint at the presence of the underground facility. The island seemed to stretch on endlessly, its dense foliage and treacherous terrain making the search even more challenging.

As they worked, the survivors found themselves growing increasingly paranoid. The island's psychological manipulation was taking its toll, and the lines between reality and illusion were becoming increasingly blurred. Each shadow in the forest seemed to hide a threat, and each noise felt like an omen of danger.

Max and Claire continued their search, determined to find the missing captives and uncover the truth about the island. They knew that time was running out, and the longer they waited, the more their friends would suffer.

As dusk fell over the island, the survivors gathered around the campfire, their faces etched with exhaustion and worry. Max and Claire briefed the group on their progress, sharing what little information they had gathered. The mood was somber, and the weight of their situation was heavy on their shoulders.

"We'll keep searching," Max said, his voice resolute. "We can't give up. Our friends need us."

The survivors nodded in agreement, their spirits lifted by Max's determination. Despite the fear and uncertainty, they knew they had to keep fighting. The island's dangers were ever-present, but they had to find a way to overcome them.

As the night wore on, the survivors tried to rest, but sleep was elusive. The island's eerie atmosphere and the constant threat of danger kept them on edge. The psychological warfare was relentless, and the survivors were forced to confront their deepest fears and insecurities.

In the underground facility, the captives were subjected to a new round of psychological tests. The memory stimulator was used to probe their minds, extracting their deepest fears and anxieties. The tests were designed to break their spirits and force them to confront the horrors of their own minds.

Anna and Ethan struggled to maintain their sanity as the tests continued. The memories they had cherished were twisted and distorted, leaving them questioning their own perceptions.

The facility was a place of nightmares, and the captives were trapped in a web of psychological torment.

As the hours dragged on, the captives grew more desperate. They tried to piece together any information that might help them escape, but the facility's harsh environment made it difficult. The experiments were designed to break them down, and the captives were forced to confront their darkest fears.

Back at the camp, Max and Claire continued their search, their determination unwavering. They knew that finding the underground facility was crucial to their survival, and they were willing to risk everything to rescue their friends.

The survivors' journey was far from over, and the challenges they faced were only growing more intense. The island was a hostile environment, and the psychological warfare was taking its toll on their minds and spirits.

As dawn approached, Max and Claire gathered the survivors for another day of searching. They were tired and worn, but their resolve remained strong. They knew that their friends' lives depended on their success, and they were determined to find a way to rescue them.

The island's secrets were beginning to unravel, but the true nature of the experiment remained elusive. The survivors were trapped in a nightmarish scenario, and the only way out was to confront the forces controlling their fate.

Max and the others pressed on, their spirits buoyed by the hope of rescuing their friends and uncovering the truth. The island was a place of darkness and danger, but they were determined to fight back and reclaim their lives.

The battle for survival was far from over, and the island's psychological manipulation was only beginning to reveal its true horrors. The survivors had to stay vigilant and united if they were to overcome the challenges that lay ahead and find a way to escape the island's deadly grasp.

Chapter 7: Escape Plans

Max stood at the edge of the forest clearing, the weight of their recent discovery settling heavily on his shoulders. The realization that they were part of an advanced psychological experiment was a bitter pill to swallow. The encrypted documents, the mysterious bunkers, and the increasingly bizarre occurrences on the island had pointed towards it, but seeing it with his own eyes had made it all too real.

"Are we sure about this?" asked Lisa, her voice trembling slightly. She had been one of the few who had managed to maintain her composure, but even she was visibly shaken now.

"There's no doubt," Max replied firmly. "The evidence we've gathered points directly to 'Project Horizon.' It's a military experiment designed to push human survival instincts to their limits. They've manipulated our memories, kept us isolated, and subjected us to constant psychological stress."

The survivors had taken refuge in a hidden bunker they had discovered weeks earlier. The bunker had been their sanctuary, a place where they could regroup and plan their next steps. But now, it felt like a temporary reprieve from a larger nightmare.

The group was gathered around a makeshift table, strewn with documents, maps, and electronic equipment salvaged from the bunkers. Max had called an urgent meeting to discuss their next move, aware that they needed to act quickly before the psychological games escalated further.

"Max, if this is all true, what do we do now?" asked Claire, her voice filled with a mix of frustration and desperation. Claire had been a nurse on the flight, and her practical nature had made her a valuable asset in their survival efforts.

"We need to confront Alex," Max said decisively. "He's been acting suspiciously ever since we found the first bunker. We need to find out if he's part of this experiment or if he's working with the people behind it."

Alex had become a polarizing figure among the survivors. He had questioned Max's leadership, challenged his decisions, and made cryptic remarks about the island's true nature. While some believed Alex was simply trying to secure a position of power, Max had become increasingly convinced that there was more to his behavior than met the eye.

As the group prepared to leave the bunker, Max and a few trusted members made their way towards Alex's camp. The air was thick with tension. Every rustle of leaves and distant sound was magnified by their heightened senses, a side effect of the psychological manipulation they had been subjected to.

The journey to Alex's camp was uneventful, but the atmosphere was charged with a sense of impending confrontation. When they arrived, they found Alex seated by a small fire, his back turned to them.

"Alex, we need to talk," Max said, his voice stern.

Alex turned slowly, a casual expression on his face. "Ah, Max. I've been expecting you."

The tone was nonchalant, but Max could see the glint of calculation in Alex's eyes. "What's this about, Alex? We've found out about 'Project Horizon.' We know this island is part of a military experiment. Are you involved in this?"

Alex's face remained impassive for a moment before he chuckled softly. "So, you've figured it out. I suppose I shouldn't be surprised. It was only a matter of time."

Max's eyes narrowed. "You're not denying it then?"

"Not at all," Alex said, rising from his seat. "In fact, I've been trying to figure out how to tell you all. But I suppose the situation calls for a different approach."

Claire stepped forward, her expression a mixture of anger and disbelief. "Why didn't you tell us before? We could have worked together."

Alex shrugged. "I didn't trust you. The experiment is designed to test our reactions under extreme duress. Sharing information too early could have compromised the results. Besides, the experiment isn't just about survival. It's about manipulation, control. If I had revealed everything, it would have skewed the outcomes."

Max felt a surge of frustration. "So you've been playing your own game while we've been struggling to survive?"

Alex's smile was wry. "Not exactly. I've been trying to gather information, just like you. The experiment's creators are watching us closely. They want to see how we react to pressure, deception, and betrayal."

"Then why are you helping us now?" Lisa asked, her voice tinged with skepticism.

"Because the situation has changed," Alex replied. "The experiment is reaching its final stages, and the stakes are higher than ever. We need to work together if we want any chance of escaping this nightmare."

Max studied Alex's face, trying to gauge his sincerity. "What's your endgame, Alex? Are you looking to escape with us, or do you have another agenda?"

"I have my own plans," Alex admitted. "But I'm willing to collaborate for now. We need to focus on disabling the drones and taking control of the technology. It's the only way we'll get out of here."

The group exchanged glances, weighing Alex's words. Despite their mistrust, they knew that their options were limited. If they wanted to escape, they needed to act quickly.

Max took a deep breath. "Alright, Alex. We'll work together for now. But if you double-cross us, I promise you'll regret it."

Alex's smile widened slightly. "Understood. Let's get to work."

As the group set out to implement their plan, Max couldn't shake the feeling that they were walking a fine line. The experiment had pushed them to their limits, and now they were on the brink of a crucial phase. Every decision, every action, would be scrutinized by the unseen forces controlling the island.

The survivors' mission was clear: disable the drones and hijack the technology to create a way off the island. But with Alex's uncertain motives and the ever-present threat of psychological manipulation, success was far from guaranteed.

Max led the team to a secluded location where they could begin their plan. The bunker had provided them with the necessary equipment and information, but the execution would be the real challenge.

They worked diligently, setting up equipment and preparing for the task ahead. Each member of the team played a crucial role, their skills and expertise coming together to form a cohesive plan. The stakes were high, and failure was not an option.

As night fell, the group was ready to put their plan into action. The darkness offered cover, but it also heightened their sense of vulnerability. The island's atmosphere was charged with anticipation, the oppressive weight of their situation palpable.

Max took one last look at the group before they moved out. "Stay sharp. We don't know what to expect, but we need to be prepared for anything."

With that, they set out into the night, their determination fueling their every step. The island was a maze of shadows and uncertainty, but they were driven by a shared goal: escape.

The journey ahead would be fraught with challenges, but Max and the survivors were ready to face whatever lay ahead. The experiment had pushed them to their limits, but they were determined to break free from its grasp and find a way back to the world they once knew.

And so, with resolve in their hearts and the shadow of the experiment looming over them, they embarked on their mission, hoping that their efforts would be enough to secure their freedom.

Max paced back and forth within the confines of their temporary base, a crude shelter formed from salvaged materials and palm fronds. The oppressive heat of the island, compounded by the ever-present humidity, seemed to cling to him like a second skin. His mind raced with the implications of their newfound knowledge. The island was not an accidental destination but a meticulously engineered trap designed to test their limits.

Around him, a small group of survivors, the ones who had been with him through the most harrowing experiences, were gathered. Their faces were etched with exhaustion and apprehension. They had finally come to terms with the fact that their predicament was far more sinister than a mere plane crash. They were participants in "Project Horizon," a nefarious military experiment. The revelation had hit them like a sledgehammer, shaking their understanding of reality.

Max looked at Lily, the medical student whose calm demeanor had been a source of reassurance to the group. She was meticulously examining the advanced equipment they had discovered in the bunker, trying to make sense of its components. Beside her, was Tom, the ex-marine who had become one of Max's closest allies. He was poring over the encrypted files they had recovered, attempting to decipher their contents.

"What's the status on the drones?" Max asked Tom, his voice barely concealing his urgency.

Tom looked up from his laptop, his brow furrowed in concentration. "We've identified their frequencies and patterns, but disabling them is going to be a challenge. They're equipped with advanced countermeasures."

Max nodded, running a hand through his hair. "We need to act quickly. The longer we stay here, the more dangerous it becomes. If Alex and his faction get wind of our plan, they'll try to sabotage it."

Lily glanced up from her work, her eyes reflecting a mix of determination and worry. "Have you figured out how to use the technology we found? Can it help us?"

Max took a deep breath and nodded. "We've got access to some powerful equipment. If we can harness it properly, we might be able to turn the tables on the drones. But first, we need to secure the area and make sure Alex doesn't catch wind of what we're planning."

Tom slammed the laptop shut, frustration evident on his face. "Alex is becoming a bigger problem than we anticipated. He's not just a civilian; he's a wildcard who's been playing both sides."

Max's eyes narrowed. "We have to be smart about this. We need to outmaneuver him and his faction without drawing too much attention. If we can disable the drones and hijack the technology, we might have a chance to get off this island."

The group fell into a tense silence, each person contemplating the gravity of their situation. The dream of escape seemed tantalizingly close, yet so far out of reach.

As the sun began to set, casting long shadows over the makeshift camp, the survivors prepared for the task ahead. They had managed to locate several drones flying overhead, their ominous presence a constant reminder of the experiment's watchful eye. The plan was to set up a temporary base near one of the bunkers, use the equipment to disrupt the drones' signals, and then attempt to communicate with the outside world.

The group split into teams. Max and Tom would handle the technical aspects, while Lily and a few others would focus on reconnaissance and security. The tension was palpable as they moved out, each step heavy with the weight of uncertainty and fear.

Max and Tom arrived at the bunker, which had been partially buried in the sand and overgrown with vegetation. The entrance was hidden, almost camouflaged by the surrounding foliage. They pried open the door, revealing a dark, metallic interior that smelled faintly of rust and decay.

Inside, the bunker was filled with an array of advanced equipment, the likes of which Max had never seen before. Screens flickered with encrypted data, and rows of high-tech gadgets were neatly arranged on shelves. Tom immediately went to work, connecting a portable device to one of the main consoles.

"This is going to take a while," Tom said, his fingers flying over the keys. "We need to crack the encryption and gain access to the drone control systems."

Max nodded, his eyes scanning the room for anything else that might be useful. He found a large map of the island with marked locations and various symbols that made his pulse quicken. The map detailed the drone flight paths and possible locations of additional bunkers.

"This map could be crucial," Max said, unfolding it carefully. "If we can figure out their full coverage, we might be able to find blind spots."

Tom glanced up, wiping sweat from his brow. "Good find. Let's use this to our advantage."

As Tom continued working on the console, Max studied the map intently. The island was covered with a network of drones, but there were several areas marked with red symbols.

These could potentially be weak points in the drones' coverage, or perhaps locations where additional equipment was stored.

Lily and her team returned from their reconnaissance mission, reporting that they had seen Alex's faction setting up their own base camp not far from the main area. The group's distrust and paranoia were evident, with Alex increasingly isolating himself from the rest of the survivors.

"We've got to be careful," Lily said, her voice low. "Alex's people are not only a threat but also unpredictable. They might try to sabotage our efforts if they find out what we're doing."

Max glanced at the clock. They had only a few hours before nightfall, and time was running out. "We need to complete our setup before dark. Once the drones start their patrols, it'll be even harder to move around."

Tom's fingers paused for a moment. "I've managed to crack part of the encryption. We've got access to the drone frequencies, but we need to override their security protocols to disable them."

Max frowned. "How long will that take?"

"Given the complexity, at least another hour," Tom replied, sweat trickling down his face.

Max nodded, understanding the urgency. "Let's move quickly. Lily, start setting up a perimeter around the bunker. We don't want any surprises."

The group worked feverishly, setting up makeshift defenses and ensuring their operations remained hidden. The sun dipped below the horizon, casting the island into darkness. The air grew cooler, but the tension remained high.

As they neared completion, Max's thoughts drifted to Alex and his faction. They had to remain vigilant. Alex was a wildcard, and his motivations were becoming increasingly unclear. Was he part of the experiment, or was he simply another survivor trying to survive by any means necessary?

The thought gnawed at Max, but he pushed it aside. For now, their focus was on disabling the drones and finding a way off the island. As Tom worked on the final stages of the override, Max's mind raced with strategies and contingencies. They had one chance to get this right.

Finally, Tom gave a weary nod. "We're ready. I've managed to disable a significant portion of their drones. We should have a window of opportunity now."

Max exhaled deeply, a mixture of relief and apprehension washing over him. "Good work. Let's move quickly. We need to seize this chance before they realize what's happening."

The group moved out of the bunker, stealthily making their way to the designated locations on the map. The plan was to disable as many drones as possible and use the momentary lapse in surveillance to establish communication with the outside world.

As they approached one of the drone control stations, Max's heart pounded in his chest. The shadows of the jungle loomed around them, and every rustle of leaves seemed amplified in the eerie silence. They had to be precise, ensuring that their actions were both swift and silent.

Lily's team took position, while Max and Tom set up the equipment necessary to hijack the drone technology. Max's hands trembled slightly as he worked, but he forced himself to stay focused. The stakes were too high.

Minutes ticked by, each second feeling like an eternity. The drones, previously a constant presence, were now sporadically patrolling the skies. Their movements were erratic, providing the group with a much-needed opportunity.

Tom's device beeped, signaling that they had successfully overridden the drone control systems in the area. "It's working. We've got control over several drones in this sector."

Max nodded, signaling Lily to start the communication process. They had to make contact with anyone who might be able to help them. The realization that they were potentially just one step away from escape spurred them into action.

The group worked tirelessly through the night, making the most of the temporary lapse in surveillance. Their efforts were a race against time, knowing that the experiment's controllers would soon realize what was happening.

As dawn approached, the group returned to their makeshift base, exhausted but hopeful. The temporary victory was a small glimmer of hope in their dire situation. However, the underlying tension remained. Alex's faction was still a significant threat, and they needed to be prepared for any eventuality.

Max gathered the group for a brief meeting, his expression serious. "We've made progress, but this is just the beginning. Alex and his faction are still out there, and we can't let our guard down. We need to stay focused and continue our efforts to escape."

Lily nodded, her face reflecting the strain of their ordeal. "We'll keep monitoring the drones and continue working on the communication systems. We need to be ready for any changes."

Tom added, "I'll keep working on the encryption and see if we can gain further access to the control systems. We need to stay ahead of the experiment's controllers."

The group dispersed, each member taking on their assigned tasks. The oppressive heat of the island seemed to intensify, but they were driven by a renewed sense of purpose. Their fight for survival was far from over, but the glimmer of hope they had achieved was a vital step towards their ultimate goal.

As Max looked out over the island, he couldn't shake the feeling that they were still only scratching the surface of the experiment's true nature. The island held many secrets, and they were yet to uncover the full extent of the psychological warfare they were entangled in.

The battle for survival was far from over, and the stakes were higher than ever. The group had to remain vigilant, for the true nature of their situation was more complex and dangerous than they had ever imagined.

Chapter 8: Betrayal

Max sat in the dimly lit bunker, the air thick with tension and the faint hum of the equipment they had managed to repurpose. The once-hidden room had become the focal point of their efforts to escape the island. Maps and technical readouts were scattered across makeshift tables, and the survivors moved with a mix of urgency and fatigue.

Tom was hunched over a laptop, his fingers flying over the keyboard as he worked to crack more of the encrypted files. Lily and her small team were busy fortifying their defenses, setting up makeshift barricades and keeping watch. Despite their progress, Max couldn't shake the nagging sense that something was terribly wrong. The atmosphere was charged with a palpable unease, one that had only deepened since the revelation of the experiment's true nature.

As Max reviewed the information Tom had deciphered, a troubling thought crossed his mind. The security of their temporary base had been compromised multiple times, and while they had initially chalked it up to the dangers of the island, a more sinister possibility began to take shape. Someone within their group might be feeding information to the unseen forces controlling the island.

The door to the bunker creaked open, and Alex strode in, his expression as inscrutable as ever. He had become increasingly antagonistic toward Max, and their strained interactions had only added to the group's tension. Alex's arrival was often marked by a palpable shift in the room's dynamics—an undercurrent of hostility that seemed to follow him.

"Any progress on disabling more drones?" Alex asked, his tone carrying a note of impatience.

Max looked up from the map he was studying. "We've made some headway, but we're still far from where we need to be. Tom's working on cracking more of the encrypted files."

Alex nodded, but Max noticed a flicker of something in his eyes—an unreadable emotion that made Max's skin crawl. He had tried to keep his distrust in check, but the recent incidents had only fueled his suspicions.

"Have you heard anything about a mole?" Alex's voice was casual, but there was a hint of something else beneath the surface.

Max's gaze narrowed. "What do you mean?"

Alex shrugged. "Just a rumor. I overheard some talk about someone possibly betraying us."

Max's heart skipped a beat. The idea of a traitor within their ranks was both terrifying and infuriating. "If you know something, you should tell us. We can't afford any more secrets."

Alex's eyes met Max's with a cold, unreadable stare. "I don't have any solid proof, just a feeling. But it might be worth looking into."

Max felt a chill run down his spine. He had hoped to avoid more internal conflicts, but the thought of a mole was too significant to ignore. He turned to Tom, who had been listening intently.

"Tom, can you check the logs and see if there's any irregular activity?" Max asked.

Tom nodded, his face grim. "I'll get on it right away."

As Tom began sifting through the data, Max's mind raced with possible suspects. The thought of someone deliberately undermining their efforts was a bitter pill to swallow. They had already faced so many external threats—now, the possibility of betrayal from within felt like the final blow.

The bunker's tense silence was broken by Lily, who entered with a worried expression. "Max, we've had some issues with our perimeter defenses. It looks like someone tampered with the setup."

Max's jaw tightened. "This is getting out of hand. We need to address this immediately."

He gathered the survivors in the bunker, calling for an emergency meeting. The group assembled with a mix of curiosity and anxiety, each person casting furtive glances at one another. The atmosphere was thick with suspicion, and Max could feel the weight of unspoken accusations.

"We've had a security breach," Max began, his voice steady despite the turmoil within him. "There are signs that someone might be sabotaging our efforts and feeding information to the outside forces controlling this island."

A murmur of disbelief and concern rippled through the group. Max's gaze swept over their faces, looking for any sign of guilt or nervousness. Alex, standing to one side, watched with a detached expression, his arms crossed over his chest.

Lily stepped forward, her expression troubled. "If there's a mole among us, it could explain the recent incidents. We've had our perimeter defenses compromised, and there's been strange activity on our surveillance equipment."

Max nodded. "We need to find out who's responsible. This is a matter of life and death."

Tom raised his hand, his face grim. "I've been going through the logs, and there are indeed some anomalies. Certain files and data have been accessed or modified in ways that suggest someone with insider knowledge is involved."

Max felt a surge of anger and frustration. The idea of a traitor within their ranks was a blow to their already fragile unity. "We need to conduct a thorough investigation. Anyone who's been involved in handling sensitive information or accessing restricted areas should come forward."

The group exchanged uneasy glances, each person weighing the implications of the accusation. Max could see the fear and uncertainty in their eyes, and he knew that the revelation of a mole would only deepen the fractures within their group.

Alex's voice cut through the tension. "I've been suspicious of a few people myself. It's not just about who's been sabotaging our efforts but also about who might be aligned with the forces controlling the island."

Max turned to Alex, his patience wearing thin. "Do you have any specific suspicions, or are you just trying to deflect attention from yourself?"

Alex's expression hardened. "I'm just stating what I've observed. We need to be cautious about everyone."

Max's eyes narrowed. "We need facts, not accusations. Let's focus on finding out who's responsible."

As the group began to question each other, the atmosphere grew increasingly tense. Each person's alibi was scrutinized, and trust eroded further. Max could sense the growing paranoia, and he knew that finding the mole would be crucial to their survival.

Hours passed in a blur of questioning and investigation. The group's mood was grim, and the once-cohesive unit was now fractured by suspicion and distrust. Max could feel the weight of the situation pressing down on him, and he knew that the longer they took to identify the traitor, the greater the risk to their survival.

Eventually, Tom approached Max with a grim expression. "I've found something that might help us narrow down the suspect list. The access logs show that certain individuals had unauthorized access to the bunker's systems."

Max's heart raced as he looked at the data Tom had collected. "Who are they?"

Tom pointed to a few names on the list. "These people had access to sensitive information and equipment. It's a starting point for our investigation."

Max studied the names, his mind racing. He knew that accusing someone without solid evidence could lead to further division and conflict. He had to approach the situation carefully to avoid tipping the balance further.

As the group gathered again, Max addressed them with a steely determination. "We have identified a few individuals who had unauthorized access to our systems. We need to investigate further and find out who's been betraying us."

The room fell silent as everyone absorbed the gravity of the situation. Max could see the fear and uncertainty in their eyes, and he knew that the revelation of the mole would have far-reaching consequences.

Alex's voice broke the silence. "I suggest we conduct a thorough search of everyone's belongings and personal items. If someone is hiding something, it's bound to turn up."

Max nodded in agreement. "We'll conduct the search immediately. Everyone needs to cooperate. This is the only way we'll find out who's been undermining our efforts."

The search was methodical and exhaustive, each person's belongings scrutinized for any sign of treachery. Max watched as the survivors, once allies, now eyed each other with a mix of suspicion and fear. The sense of unity that had held them together was now shattered, replaced by a gnawing distrust.

As the search continued, Lily approached Max with a worried expression. "Max, I found something unusual in one of the tents. It looks like a hidden communication device."

Max's heart sank. If someone had been using a hidden device to communicate with the forces controlling the island, it could explain many of the recent incidents. He examined the device carefully, noting its advanced technology and the fact that it had been carefully concealed.

"This could be the evidence we need," Max said, his voice tight with frustration. "We need to find out who this belongs to."

The group gathered once more, and Max held up the device for everyone to see. "We found this hidden in one of the tents. It appears to be a communication device. Does anyone recognize it?"

The room erupted into a chaotic flurry of accusations and defensive statements. The pressure of the situation had pushed everyone to their limits, and the once-cohesive group was now on the brink of disintegration.

Max's voice cut through the chaos. "We need to remain focused. The truth will come out, but we must stay united if we want to survive."

The investigation continued, and the group's paranoia reached new heights. Each person's actions were scrutinized, and the atmosphere grew increasingly hostile. Trust had become a rare commodity, and the weight of betrayal hung heavy over them.

As night fell, the tension in the bunker was almost unbearable. Max knew that the group's survival depended on finding the traitor and restoring some semblance of order. The stakes had never been higher, and the consequences of failure were dire.

The search for the mole continued, and Max could only hope that they would find the answers they needed before it was too late. The island's dangers were ever-present, and the threat of betrayal loomed large. The group's survival depended on their ability to confront the truth and overcome the divisions that threatened to tear them apart.

The clock was ticking, and Max knew that time was running out. The fight for survival was far from over, and the island held many more secrets waiting to be uncovered. The next steps would be crucial in determining their fate, and Max was determined to see it through to the end, no matter the cost.

The discovery of the hidden communication device sent a ripple of unease through the survivors. Max gathered the group in the bunker, his expression grim as he addressed the assembled faces. The tension was palpable, each person's gaze darting nervously around the room, the weight of suspicion hanging heavily over them.

"We found this communication device," Max began, holding up the small, sophisticated piece of technology. "It was hidden in one of the tents. It's clear that someone among us has been using it to contact the forces controlling the island."

The device, sleek and compact, emitted a faint, ominous glow. It was clear that it was not just a regular communication tool; its advanced design hinted at a level of technology far beyond what the survivors had seen so far. Max could see the mixture of fear and confusion in their eyes. The discovery of the device had only deepened their paranoia.

"I want everyone to stay calm," Max continued, trying to maintain control over the situation. "We're going to conduct a thorough search to find out who this belongs to. No one is to leave this room until we've resolved this."

The survivors exchanged uneasy glances, and the air in the bunker grew thick with tension. The room was filled with a mix of frustration, fear, and anger as they began to sort through the belongings of their fellow survivors. Each person's possessions were examined meticulously, but the search yielded little immediate results.

As the hours dragged on, Max's frustration mounted. The search had turned up nothing concrete, and the group's morale was visibly declining. The device's presence had thrown the survivors into a state of paranoia, with accusations flying and trust eroding with each passing moment.

In the midst of the search, Lily approached Max with a look of distress. "Max, I've been going through the supplies and found something strange. There's a hidden compartment in the storage room. It looks like it's been used recently."

Max's heart sank. If someone had been using a hidden compartment, it could mean they were trying to hide something crucial. "Show me."

They made their way to the storage room, a small, cluttered space filled with supplies and equipment. Lily pointed to a section of the wall that seemed out of place. With a bit of effort, Max managed to pry open the hidden compartment. Inside, he found a small, locked box. The box was covered in dust, suggesting it had been hidden for some time.

Max opened the box, revealing a stack of documents and a few personal items. Among the papers were several detailed maps of the island, along with a notebook filled with scribbled notes. As Max leafed through the pages, he found detailed observations and comments about the group's activities, as well as notes on the island's layout.

"This is important," Max said, holding up the notebook. "It looks like someone has been keeping detailed records of our movements and plans."

The discovery added another layer of complexity to their situation. Not only was there a mole, but this person had been meticulously documenting their every move. Max's mind raced as he tried to piece together the implications of this new information.

Returning to the main bunker, Max gathered everyone again. "We've found more evidence. This notebook and the maps suggest that whoever is betraying us has been monitoring our every move."

The group's anxiety reached new heights. Everyone's faces were etched with worry as they struggled to come to terms with the reality of their situation. The idea that someone had been actively working against them from within was a blow that shattered the group's already fragile unity.

"We need to find out who this notebook belongs to," Max said, his voice steady despite the turmoil inside him. "This is our best lead to uncovering the mole's identity."

As they examined the documents, Tom's face grew pale. "These notes... they include observations about me. It seems like someone has been paying close attention to my work."

Tom's revelation caused a ripple of suspicion to shift towards him. Max quickly intervened. "We need to remain objective. We're not pointing fingers without solid evidence."

The group continued to search through the remaining belongings, but the mood was now one of palpable distrust. The once-cohesive group was now fractured by suspicion and fear. Each person's actions and words were scrutinized with a level of intensity that bordered on paranoia.

Hours passed with little progress, and the survivors' nerves were frayed. Max's leadership was under increasing pressure as the group's cohesion continued to deteriorate. With each passing moment, the reality of their situation became more daunting.

The sound of a distant explosion startled everyone, causing a collective gasp. The ground trembled slightly, and the bunker's lights flickered. Max and the others exchanged worried glances, realizing that the explosion might be related to the unseen forces controlling the island.

"What was that?" Lily asked, her voice trembling.

"I don't know," Max replied, his mind racing. "But it might be related to the drones or the experiment."

They rushed outside to assess the situation. The explosion had caused a small fire in the distance, sending up plumes of smoke. Max, Lily, and Tom hurried to investigate, hoping to find clues that might explain the disturbance.

As they approached the source of the explosion, they found a partially destroyed drone lying among the wreckage. It was evident that the drone had been taken down by some sort of projectile, possibly one of their own makeshift weapons. Nearby, a charred piece of equipment caught Max's eye—it looked like a tracking device.

"This device... it's similar to the one we found before," Max said, holding it up. "It must have been used to track our movements."

The realization hit hard. If the drones and tracking devices were connected, it meant the forces controlling the island were closely monitoring their every action. The survivors' attempts to disable the drones and signal for help were being thwarted by a sophisticated tracking system.

"Let's get back to the bunker," Max instructed. "We need to regroup and come up with a new plan. We can't keep going in circles like this."

Back in the bunker, the mood was somber. The discovery of the tracking device had added a new layer of complexity to their situation. The survivors were now acutely aware that their attempts to escape or fight back were being carefully monitored and manipulated.

Max gathered the group for a final meeting. "We've learned that the island's forces are using tracking devices to monitor our movements. The explosion was likely a result of our attempts to disable the drones. We need to reassess our strategy."

Alex, who had been largely silent throughout the ordeal, finally spoke up. "If we're being tracked, we need to find a way to disrupt their monitoring system. We can't rely on just disabling drones; we need to think bigger."

Max nodded in agreement. "We need to find a way to jam their signals or disrupt their tracking system. It might give us the window we need to make a more decisive move."

The survivors began to brainstorm ideas, their focus shifting to finding a solution to their predicament. The group's unity was tenuous at best, but the shared goal of escaping the island brought them together in a renewed effort.

As the night wore on, Max couldn't shake the feeling of impending doom. The island was a treacherous place, and the forces controlling it were relentless. The discovery of the tracking device and the explosion were stark reminders of the danger they faced.

The survivors knew that their time was running out. The island's mysterious forces were always one step ahead, and their attempts to fight back seemed futile in the face of such overwhelming control.

Max and his team worked tirelessly to develop a plan to disrupt the tracking system. They knew that their survival depended on their ability to outsmart the forces controlling the island and find a way to escape. The stakes were higher than ever, and the pressure was mounting with each passing hour.

As dawn approached, the survivors were exhausted but determined. The island was a hostile environment, and the forces controlling it were determined to keep them trapped.

But Max and the others were not ready to give up. They had come too far and sacrificed too much to back down now.

The coming days would be critical. The survivors needed to stay focused and united if they were to have any hope of escaping the island and uncovering the truth behind the experiment. The odds were against them, but their resolve was unwavering.

The search for the mole had not yielded immediate results, but the discovery of the tracking device had provided a crucial clue. Max knew that finding and disabling the tracking system was their best chance of breaking free from the island's grasp.

As the sun rose over the horizon, Max gathered the survivors once more. The time for action was now. They had to put their plan into motion and take the fight to the forces controlling the island. The stakes were high, and the risk was enormous, but their determination to survive and escape was stronger than ever.

The battle for survival was far from over. The island held many more secrets and dangers, and the forces controlling it were not going to make their escape easy. But Max and the survivors were ready to face whatever challenges lay ahead. The fight for freedom and truth had only just begun.

Chapter 9: The Final Stand

Max stared at the smoldering remains of the bunker, his mind racing with the gravity of their situation. The discovery of the hidden tracking device had shocked everyone. It meant their every move had been monitored, every plan scrutinized by the unseen forces controlling the island. The once faint hope of escape had been dashed, replaced by the grim reality of their complete isolation.

The group assembled in the clearing, their faces etched with exhaustion and fear. The air was thick with tension as they gathered around Max, who had taken charge in the wake of the latest revelation. The stark contrast between their previous optimism and the current despair was palpable. Max knew that the only way to regain control was to confront the harsh truth head-on.

"Alright," Max began, his voice steady despite the turmoil inside. "We need to face the facts. We've been completely cut off from the outside world. This tracking device proves it. Our attempts to signal for help have been futile. We're on our own."

A murmur of agreement swept through the group, but it was clear that not everyone was ready to accept this new reality. Alex, who had been quietly observing from the sidelines, stepped forward. His face was a mixture of determination and resignation.

"So what's the plan now?" Alex asked, his tone challenging. "If we can't get a signal out, what's our next move?"

Max's eyes locked onto Alex's, reading the underlying hostility in his question. Despite their uneasy truce, there was still a deep-seated mistrust between them. Max took a deep breath before responding.

"We need to focus on the central facility," Max said firmly. "The island's main control center is our best shot at dismantling the experiment. We've seen the bunkers and the technology they hold. If we can get to the control center, we might be able to disrupt their operations and create a chance for ourselves."

The mention of the control center sparked a mix of hope and apprehension among the survivors. The central facility was known to be heavily guarded and surrounded by sophisticated security systems. The idea of infiltrating it was daunting, but it was their only viable option.

"What makes you think we can actually get in there?" one of the survivors, a young woman named Sarah, asked. Her voice trembled slightly, revealing her fear. "They've been one step ahead of us the whole time. How do we even begin to counter that?"

Max glanced at the others, gauging their reactions. "We have to rely on what we know and what we've found. The bunkers have given us valuable information about their technology and security measures. If we use that knowledge strategically, we might have a chance."

As the survivors absorbed Max's words, a sense of grim determination settled over them. They were trapped, with their every move monitored, but they still had a chance to fight back. The realization brought a renewed sense of purpose.

"We need a plan," Max continued. "A detailed one. We'll split into smaller teams. One team will focus on creating a diversion, drawing the guards away from the facility. The other team will approach the control center and attempt to gain access."

The survivors nodded, their expressions a mixture of resolve and apprehension. Max assigned roles based on the skills and strengths of each person. Alex was reluctantly given a key role in the diversion team, despite the lingering distrust between him and Max.

"Let's get to work," Max said, his voice resolute. "We don't have time to waste. Every second counts."

The survivors dispersed, each team focusing on their assigned tasks. Max and his team worked tirelessly, using the information from the bunkers to strategize their approach. The plan was risky and fraught with danger, but it was their best chance at survival.

As night fell, the island seemed eerily silent. The usual sounds of the jungle were muted, and the survivors' preparations took on a sense of urgency. Max felt the weight of their situation pressing down on him. The stakes were higher than ever, and their success depended on every detail of the plan.

Hours later, the diversion team executed their part of the plan with precision. Explosions and disturbances created chaos around the island, drawing the guards away from the central facility. Max's team seized the opportunity, making their way towards the control center.

The journey to the control center was fraught with obstacles. The security measures were more sophisticated than they had anticipated, and the group had to navigate through a maze of sensors and alarms. Each step was a gamble, with the risk of discovery looming over them.

As they approached the control center, Max's heart pounded in his chest. The facility loomed before them, a monolithic structure surrounded by high-tech barriers. The sight of it was both intimidating and exhilarating. They were so close to their goal, but the danger was far from over.

Max and his team carefully disabled the security systems one by one, using the knowledge they had gathered from the bunkers. Their movements were deliberate and calculated, each action aimed at ensuring their success. The control center's entrance was finally within reach, and Max felt a surge of hope.

However, just as they were about to breach the facility, an unexpected obstacle emerged. A series of high-pitched alarms blared, signaling that their presence had been detected. The facility's security systems had been triggered, and the survivors were thrust into a desperate race against time.

"Move!" Max shouted, his voice urgent. "We have to get inside before they lock us out!"

The team sprinted towards the entrance, their adrenaline fueling their every move. The alarms were deafening, and the intensity of the situation heightened with each passing second. They reached the control center's door, but it was locked tight, with no immediate way to open it.

Max's mind raced as he searched for a solution. The security systems were more advanced than he had anticipated, and their plan was rapidly unraveling. He needed to think quickly if they were to have any chance of succeeding.

"Cover me!" Max ordered, as he attempted to hack into the door's security system using equipment they had salvaged from the bunkers. The team provided cover, fending off any guards that approached while Max worked.

The seconds ticked by like hours, and Max could feel the pressure mounting. Sweat dripped down his face as he worked feverishly, trying to bypass the security protocols. The sound of approaching footsteps grew louder, and the team's situation became increasingly dire.

With a final, decisive keystroke, the door's lock mechanism clicked open. Max let out a breath of relief as the door swung open, revealing the interior of the control center. The team quickly moved inside, seeking refuge from the alarms and the increasing number of guards.

The control center was a sprawling, high-tech facility, filled with screens, terminals, and control panels. The sheer scale of the operation was overwhelming, and the realization of what they were up against hit Max with full force.

"Find the main control room!" Max shouted to his team. "We need to shut this place down before it's too late!"

The survivors split up, each team member tasked with locating and disabling the central control systems. Max moved through the facility with determination, driven by the knowledge that their survival depended on the success of their mission.

As they navigated through the labyrinthine corridors, Max and his team encountered more obstacles. The security measures were relentless, with automated defenses and armed guards patrolling the area. Each confrontation was a test of their resolve and skill.

Despite the challenges, the team made steady progress. They located the main control room and began working on disabling the central systems. The process was intricate and complex, requiring careful manipulation of the facility's technology.

Max's heart raced as he oversaw the operation. The control center's systems began to falter, their shutdown process unfolding before his eyes. The countdown to destruction had begun, and the survivors' hope for escape was now intertwined with the success of their mission.

As the control systems began to malfunction, the facility's alarms intensified, and the structure began to tremble. The island's infrastructure was starting to collapse, signaling the beginning of a new phase in their desperate fight for survival.

Max and his team continued their work with unwavering focus, knowing that their actions would determine the outcome of their struggle. The stakes were higher than ever, and every second counted as they raced against the clock to complete their mission.

The facility's central control room was now in disarray, with systems failing and alarms blaring. The survivors had done their part, but their journey was far from over. The island's destruction was imminent, and the final confrontation loomed large.

Max and his team regrouped, their faces reflecting the exhaustion and determination that had driven them through their ordeal. The next phase of their escape plan was crucial, and they needed to move quickly to ensure their survival.

With the control center in turmoil, the survivors prepared for the final leg of their journey. The fight for their lives was far from over, and the outcome of their struggle remained uncertain. But in that moment, Max held onto a sliver of hope, driven by the belief that they could overcome the odds and escape the island's grasp.

The battle was far from won, and the true extent of the experiment's consequences was yet to be fully revealed. But Max and his team were determined to see their mission through to the end, no matter the cost.

As they moved forward, the survivors faced their greatest challenge yet, with the island's destruction hanging over them like a dark cloud. The final stand was approaching, and the fate of everyone involved rested on their shoulders.

The clock was ticking, and the pressure was mounting. Max knew that their next steps would be critical in determining their ultimate survival. The fight for freedom was far from over, and the true test of their resolve was just beginning.

The night was thick with tension as Max and his team approached the imposing structure of the island's central facility. The dark sky, punctuated by the occasional flash of distant lightning, seemed to press down on them, heavy with the weight of their grim task. The facility loomed ahead, a monstrous edifice of steel and concrete, its stark silhouette barely discernible against the roiling clouds.

Max, leading the small group, glanced back at his companions—Sam, Lila, and Josh. Each bore the same look of grim determination. They had agreed on this mission because it was their only hope of ending the nightmare. The others would create a diversion to draw the remaining security forces away from the central facility, giving Max and his team the opportunity to infiltrate the core of the experiment.

Max adjusted his night-vision goggles and signaled for the group to move forward. The facility was equipped with high-tech security measures, but they had managed to acquire some of the facility's access codes from the bunkers they had previously explored. Now, it was a matter of navigating through the complex maze of surveillance and barriers.

They approached the facility's outer perimeter, where a high chain-link fence topped with razor wire stood between them and their objective. Max crouched beside the fence and motioned for Sam to handle the cutting tools they had scavenged. Sam worked quickly, her hands steady despite the gravity of their situation. The fence's metal groaned softly as it was sliced open, just wide enough for them to slip through.

Once inside the perimeter, they took a moment to regroup and reassess. The facility's lights flickered intermittently, casting eerie shadows on the ground. The group moved cautiously, avoiding the sporadic patrols of armed guards. The hum of machinery and the occasional beep of electronic devices provided a constant backdrop of noise, masking their footsteps.

The entrance to the facility was heavily guarded, with surveillance cameras mounted at strategic points and motion sensors on the ground. Max's heart pounded in his chest as he approached the entrance, aware that a single misstep could alert the entire facility. He held up a hand, signaling the team to halt, and pulled out the stolen access codes.

Josh took the lead in hacking the electronic lock. Sweat beaded on his forehead as he worked, his fingers flying over the small, portable device they had been using to bypass security systems. After several tense minutes, the lock clicked open, and the door creaked ajar.

The group slipped through the entrance and found themselves in a dimly lit hallway. The facility's interior was stark and clinical, with cold, metallic walls and flickering fluorescent lights. Max led the way, guiding the team through the labyrinthine corridors. They passed numerous doors, some marked with red warning signs, others with seemingly innocuous labels.

Their objective was to reach the central control room, where the main control center for the experiment was located. According to the information they had gathered, this room was the nerve center of the operation, controlling everything from surveillance to the psychological manipulation they had endured.

As they navigated the facility, Max felt a growing sense of urgency. They had little time before the diversion team would be overwhelmed, and their chance to complete the mission would be lost. The corridor ahead was blocked by a security checkpoint, a small room with a guard stationed inside.

Max signaled for the team to halt and assessed their options. He motioned for Lila to deploy the small smoke grenades they had brought along. With practiced precision, Lila lobbed the grenades into the checkpoint room. The smoke quickly filled the space, obscuring the view and causing confusion.

The guard inside stumbled into the thickening smoke, his shouts muffled by the fog. Max and his team used the distraction to slip past the checkpoint, moving quickly but quietly. They could hear the muffled sounds of the guard's radio, interspersed with the crackling of static. They had to move fast; their window of opportunity was shrinking.

Finally, they reached a large set of double doors, marked with a prominent sign reading "AUTHORIZED PERSONNEL ONLY." Max's heart raced as he pulled out the final set of access codes, hoping they would work. With a deep breath, he entered the codes into the keypad. The doors slid open with a soft hiss.

Inside the control room, rows of consoles and screens stretched out before them. The room was filled with the soft glow of computer monitors, and the hum of machinery created a constant background noise. Max could see various control panels and workstations, each monitoring different aspects of the experiment.

The team spread out, quickly working to locate the central control interface. Max approached the primary console, where a complex array of controls and data readouts were displayed. He had seen something similar in the bunkers and had a basic understanding of how to operate it.

As Max worked to access the system, Sam kept watch, her eyes darting around the room for any signs of approaching guards. The tension was palpable; any moment now, their diversion team might be overwhelmed, and their mission could be compromised.

Max's fingers flew over the keyboard as he navigated through the facility's control system. He accessed several files and discovered detailed schematics of the island's infrastructure. The information was overwhelming, but he quickly focused on finding the main control hub for the experiment.

He finally located the system that controlled the psychological manipulation and surveillance equipment. With a few quick commands, Max initiated a sequence to override the system's controls and trigger a shutdown. The facility's lights flickered and dimmed as the system began to respond.

Suddenly, a loud alarm blared throughout the facility, and red warning lights flashed. Max's heart sank. They had been discovered. The control room's doors burst open, and several armed guards stormed in, their weapons trained on the team.

"Move!" Max shouted, grabbing Sam and pulling her toward a side exit. Lila and Josh followed closely behind. They raced through the facility, the alarms blaring and the sound of heavy footsteps echoing through the corridors. The guards' shouts and the clatter of their equipment added to the chaos.

As they reached a maintenance shaft, Max saw one of their team members—Josh—was missing. He turned to look back but saw Josh lying on the ground, struggling to fend off the guards. "Go!" Josh yelled, urging the rest of the team to escape.

Without a moment's hesitation, Max and the others scrambled into the maintenance shaft. They climbed through the narrow space, their movements swift and desperate. The sound of gunfire and shouting grew fainter as they moved further away from the central control room.

Finally, they emerged on the other side of the facility, their breaths coming in ragged gasps. Max looked back at the facility, now a scene of chaos and destruction. The central control room was ablaze, the fire spreading rapidly through the facility's infrastructure.

They had succeeded in their mission, but at a great cost. Josh's sacrifice had allowed them to escape, but the weight of his loss hung heavy on Max and the others. They had to regroup and find a way to signal the diversion team and make their final escape from the island.

As they made their way back to the rendezvous point, Max reflected on the events that had transpired. The true scope of the experiment had become clearer—an advanced psychological manipulation operation funded by a shadowy multinational corporation. Their survival had been a test, and the stakes had never been higher.

With the facility in flames behind them, the team pressed on, determined to complete their escape and uncover the full extent of the conspiracy that had ensnared them.

Chapter 10: The Conspiracy

The survivors stumbled into the underground facility, a place that seemed to pulse with its own eerie, artificial life. The walls were lined with screens, blinking intermittently with streams of data that none of them could immediately understand. A large, steel door loomed in front of them, its surface marked with symbols and codes that suggested a high level of security. Max led the way, his flashlight cutting through the darkness, revealing more of the facility's hidden secrets with each step.

Inside, the air was thick with the scent of old machinery and dampness. The facility's architecture was sterile and clinical, in stark contrast to the natural chaos of the island above. The survivors spread out, their eyes darting from one piece of advanced technology to another. The dim glow from the computer screens cast an unsettling light on their faces, making their exhaustion and fear palpable.

Max approached a large console at the center of the room. It was covered in buttons, dials, and a complex array of screens. He began to type furiously, trying to access any information that might reveal the nature of their predicament. His hands shook slightly, but he forced himself to remain focused.

"Look at this," Max said, pointing to a series of encrypted files that had appeared on one of the screens. "These might give us the answers we need."

A few of the survivors gathered around, their faces lit by the screen's pale light. Among them was Dr. Jane Collins, a former neuroscientist who had previously remained silent. Her eyes widened as she scanned the files. "These documents are classified beyond anything I've ever seen," she said. "But if we can decipher them, they might tell us who's behind all this."

As Jane worked on decoding the files, another survivor, David Reynolds, discovered a series of photographs pinned to a corkboard nearby. They depicted various people—some of whom looked familiar, others not. The photos were tagged with names and dates, suggesting a meticulous and disturbing level of surveillance.

"What is this?" David asked, his voice filled with disbelief. "It looks like they've been tracking us for a long time."

Jane's eyes narrowed as she continued to analyze the files. "This is more than just an experiment," she said. "These documents point to a global network of operations. It seems we were specifically selected for this test."

A sense of dread fell over the group as they processed Jane's revelation. They were not just random victims of a cruel game—they were chosen because of their backgrounds, their weaknesses, and their potential to be manipulated.

Max turned back to the console, which was now displaying a series of schematics and operational plans. "We need to understand what's happening at a deeper level," he said. "There's got to be a central command somewhere that controls everything."

Jane nodded in agreement. "The files mention something about a 'central hub' where the main operations are coordinated. If we can find and access that hub, we might uncover the full scope of their plans."

With renewed determination, the group split up to search for this central hub. Max and a few others moved through the facility, their footsteps echoing in the empty halls. The facility was vast, its rooms filled with advanced technology and equipment that seemed to mock their efforts with its inscrutability.

After what felt like hours of searching, Max and his team found themselves in a large control room. It was dominated by a massive, circular table covered in more screens and controls. At the center was a holographic display showing a map of the island, marked with various points of interest and surveillance data.

"This is it," Max said, his voice heavy with awe and dread. "This must be the main control center."

Jane approached the holographic map, her fingers tracing the various markers. "This map shows the entire island and all the monitoring points," she said. "They've been tracking our every move."

As they continued to examine the control room, Max's eyes fell upon a series of documents displayed on a screen labeled "Project Horizon." The documents contained detailed descriptions of psychological experiments, manipulation techniques, and the use of advanced technology for mind control.

"What is this?" David asked, looking over Max's shoulder.

Max read through the documents, his expression darkening with each passing line. "It's all laid out here. Project Horizon isn't just an experiment—it's a full-scale operation designed to test and manipulate human behavior under extreme conditions."

Jane shook her head in disbelief. "This is beyond anything I imagined. They've been playing us like puppets, testing how far they can push us before we break."

The reality of their situation began to sink in. The survivors were not merely stranded; they were part of a grand, horrifying experiment conducted by a shadowy multinational corporation. Their lives had been manipulated and controlled from the beginning, their memories altered to fit the experiment's needs.

Max turned to the group, his face set in grim determination. "We need to confront the puppet masters behind this. We can't let them get away with what they've done."

Jane looked at Max with a mixture of fear and resolve. "But how do we even begin to fight an organization like this?"

Max's gaze hardened. "We find out who's in charge, and we make them pay for what they've done to us. We have to expose this operation, no matter what it takes."

With a newfound sense of purpose, the survivors prepared for their next move. They knew that their fight was far from over, but they were determined to uncover the truth and bring those responsible for their suffering to justice. As they set out to confront the puppet masters, they steeled themselves for the challenges ahead, knowing that their very survival depended on their ability to navigate the dangerous and deceptive world they had been thrust into.

The central hub of Project Horizon was more than just a facility—it was a symbol of the lengths to which the puppet masters would go to control and manipulate. But Max and the others were ready to confront the darkness that lay ahead, fueled by the knowledge that their fight was not just for their own lives, but for the truth that had been so cruelly hidden from them.

The survivors sat in stunned silence, their faces illuminated by the flickering lights of the facility's emergency generators. The files they had discovered revealed a network of deceit far beyond anything they had imagined. The shadows of their ordeal stretched out further than they could have ever anticipated.

Max, Lucy, and the others gathered around a makeshift table in what had once been a storage room but now served as their command center. The papers spread out before them were filled with technical jargon and unsettling details about the experiment they were part of. The grim realization settled in: their ordeal was not a random accident but a calculated experiment orchestrated by a powerful multinational corporation.

Max's fingers trembled slightly as he flipped through the documents, his mind racing to make sense of the staggering revelations. "This is more than just an experiment. This is a full-scale operation. They've been tracking us, manipulating us, and playing with our lives for their own gain."

Lucy, her face pale and her eyes wide with disbelief, pointed to one document that detailed the selection criteria for the experiment's subjects. "They chose us based on our backgrounds. They knew exactly who we were before we even got on that plane. This isn't just about survival—it's about control."

David, the tech-savvy member of their group, leaned in to examine a schematic diagram of the facility's network. "Look at this. The entire system is integrated. They've been monitoring every step we've taken, every move we've made. And there's more." He pointed to a section detailing experimental technologies used to manipulate emotions and perceptions. "They've been using us to test their new mind control technology."

A heavy silence fell over the group as the implications sank in. The realization that their suffering had been part of a grand scheme, orchestrated by forces far beyond their control, left them feeling both furious and powerless.

Max clenched his fists, his anger barely contained. "We need to confront them. We need to make them pay for what they've done to us."

Lucy nodded in agreement, her voice steady despite the turmoil inside her. "But we also need to find a way out of here. If they're giving us an ultimatum, we have to be prepared for whatever comes next."

Before they could formulate a plan, the door to the room creaked open, and a figure stepped inside—a tall, imposing man in a sharp suit. His face was calm, almost too calm, given the gravity of the situation. "I see you've discovered the truth," he said, his voice smooth and controlled. "I am Mr. Blackwood, and I represent the interests behind this project."

The survivors tensed, readying themselves for whatever confrontation lay ahead. Max took a step forward, his voice filled with determination. "We've seen what you're doing here. We know about the experiment and the manipulation. What's your endgame?"

Mr. Blackwood's expression remained unchanged. "Our endgame? It's quite simple. We're testing the limits of human behavior under extreme conditions. We want to understand how people react when pushed to their breaking points. Your participation has provided us with invaluable data."

David's eyes narrowed in anger. "You're talking about our lives as if they're nothing but lab rats in an experiment. This is sick."

Mr. Blackwood's gaze swept over the group, assessing their reactions. "Your indignation is understandable, but it's irrelevant to our objectives. You have a choice now: continue as overseers of this experiment or face the consequences of trying to escape."

The group exchanged uneasy glances. The notion of becoming a part of the machinery that had tormented them was abhorrent, but the alternative was equally terrifying. Max, his mind racing, weighed their options. "If we refuse to cooperate, what happens to us?"

Mr. Blackwood's eyes gleamed with a cold, unfeeling light. "You will be eliminated. The island's infrastructure is set to self-destruct if you attempt to disrupt our operations. You have twenty-four hours to make your decision. Failure to comply will result in the detonation of the control center."

The enormity of their situation struck the survivors with a fresh wave of despair. They were caught in a nightmarish trap, with no easy way out and a looming deadline hanging over them.

Max turned to his group, his resolve hardening. "We're not going to be pawns in their game. We need to find a way to sabotage their system, expose their crimes, and make sure no one else has to suffer like we did."

Lucy, her face set with determination, nodded. "We'll need to move quickly. We don't have much time to act."

David, his mind already working through the technical details, spoke up. "We'll need to disable their security systems and bypass their surveillance. It won't be easy, but if we can get to the central control room, we might be able to shut it down and escape before they can execute their threat."

The group began to formulate a plan, each member focusing on their strengths. Max and Lucy would lead the charge to infiltrate the control room, while David and others worked on disrupting the facility's security measures. Every detail had to be meticulously planned, with no room for error.

As the survivors prepared for their final confrontation with the puppet masters, the tension in the air was palpable. They knew that their survival depended not just on their ability to fight back but on their capacity to outthink and outmaneuver their ruthless captors.

The clock was ticking, and the stakes had never been higher. With a mix of fear and determination driving them, the survivors readied themselves for the ultimate battle against the forces that had twisted their lives into a cruel game of survival.

Chapter 11: The Countdown

The central control room of the island's facility was an array of blinking lights and humming machinery. The walls, lined with screens, showed a chaotic montage of surveillance feeds, tracking the survivors' every move. Each monitor displayed a different perspective—through the eyes of drones, hidden cameras, or satellite feeds. The facility had been the heart of their torment, a place where every emotion, every desperate gasp, and every failed escape attempt was catalogued and analyzed.

Max, Samantha, and the few survivors who had managed to evade capture found themselves in the room's dim light. They had been planning this moment for days, meticulously plotting their attack on the system that had become their prison. It was a final, desperate gamble—a bid to reclaim their freedom or die trying.

"Everything is set," Samantha said, her voice tight with tension. She was crouched beside a console, her fingers flying over the controls. "The self-destruct sequence is activated. We've got ten minutes before this place blows."

Max glanced at the large digital clock on the wall, which ticked down the seconds with relentless precision. The numbers were a constant reminder of the fleeting time they had left. Sweat trickled down his back, and he wiped his brow with a shaking hand. The knowledge that their plan could fail at any moment was a weight on his shoulders.

"We need to get to the escape route before the facility goes up," Max said, his voice steady despite the gravity of the situation. "Let's move."

The team of survivors, armed with the weapons they had found in the bunkers, moved swiftly through the darkened corridors. Their makeshift plan had been to disable the facility's main control center, but they hadn't anticipated how complex and fortified the system would be. Every corner of the facility seemed to be a labyrinth, filled with security measures and armed guards.

As they navigated the facility, they encountered the remnants of the facility's automated defenses. Drones, programmed to protect the facility, whizzed by, their sensors scanning for any sign of intrusion. The survivors ducked behind walls and avoided the drones' detection, their movements synchronized and cautious.

Meanwhile, the facility's overseers, the unseen puppet masters behind Project Horizon, were reacting to the breach. The room where they monitored the facility was buzzing with frantic activity. Alarms blared, and red lights flashed, signaling the emergency protocols. The puppet masters, shadowy figures whose faces remained hidden in the gloom, began issuing commands through encrypted channels.

"We can't let them interfere," Max said, his eyes scanning the monitors for any sign of additional security measures. "If they get wind of our plan, we're done for."

As the group reached the facility's main exit, they encountered an unexpected obstacle—Alex. The former ally, now fully aligned with the puppet masters, stood blocking their path. His face was set in a grim expression, and his eyes, once friendly, were now cold and calculating.

"I didn't think you'd make it this far," Alex said, his voice dripping with contempt. "But this is where it ends. You're not getting out."

Max stepped forward, his stance resolute. "We're not backing down. We've already done what we came here to do. You can't stop us."

A tense silence fell over the corridor. The survivors, their weapons drawn, watched as Max and Alex faced off. The air was thick with the weight of unspoken betrayal and conflict. Alex's allegiance to the puppet masters was a bitter pill to swallow, but it was a reality they had to confront.

Without warning, Alex lunged at Max, his weapon raised. Max, anticipating the attack, sidestepped and countered with a quick jab. The clash of metal and the grunts of exertion filled the corridor as they fought. The other survivors, caught in the crossfire, struggled to stay out of the way while also preparing for any additional threats.

Samantha, observing the fight, realized that their time was running out. The countdown on the central control room's clock continued to tick down, each second bringing them closer to the facility's destruction. She grabbed a nearby comms device and sent a distress signal, hoping it would reach anyone who might still be outside the facility and alert them to the impending disaster.

"Come on, Max!" Samantha shouted, her voice filled with urgency. "We need to go!"

Max, struggling against Alex's relentless attacks, managed to break free. He delivered a decisive blow, knocking Alex to the ground. Alex's weapon clattered away, and he looked up at Max with a mixture of rage and resignation.

"This isn't over," Alex spat, his voice tinged with defiance. "You can't win. The experiment—"

But before he could finish, a burst of static crackled through the comms device. The remaining survivors had managed to contact the outside world, alerting them to the experiment's true nature. The puppet masters, realizing their plans were falling apart, scrambled to regain control.

With Alex incapacitated, Max and the survivors made a run for the exit. The facility's corridors were in chaos, with alarms blaring and lights flashing. The facility's automated defenses, now in full alert mode, began to launch their final assault. The survivors raced through the facility, their breaths coming in ragged gasps as they navigated the maze of passages.

As they approached the escape route, they encountered a final barrier—an armored door, designed to keep intruders out. Samantha worked quickly, using the codes she had hacked from the facility's system to override the door's security. The door creaked open, revealing a darkened tunnel that led to the outside.

"Move, move!" Max urged, his voice urgent. The survivors rushed through the tunnel, their footsteps echoing off the walls. Behind them, the facility's self-destruct sequence continued its relentless countdown.

Emerging from the tunnel, the survivors found themselves on the edge of a cliff overlooking the island's tumultuous waters. The sky above was a roiling mass of dark clouds, and the sea below crashed violently against the rocks.

Max scanned the horizon, searching for any sign of a rescue. The island's chaos was a stark contrast to the calm facade that had once hidden the facility's dark secrets. The survivors' escape from the facility had been just the first step—now, they had to find a way off the island before the facility's destruction consumed them.

"Is there any sign of a boat or a way out?" Max asked, his voice strained with exhaustion.

Samantha, checking the equipment they had salvaged, shook her head. "Nothing yet. But we can't wait much longer. We need to find a way to signal for help."

The survivors, their faces marked by fear and determination, prepared for the final leg of their escape. The facility's destruction was imminent, and they had little time to find safety. As they scoured the cliffside for a potential escape route, the sound of approaching aircraft filled the air. The island's final assault was beginning.

Max turned to the group, his eyes steely with resolve. "We've come too far to give up now. We need to keep moving and find a way to escape this nightmare."

With the countdown ticking relentlessly toward zero, the survivors faced their last challenge—a race against time to escape the island's final disaster. As the facility's destruction loomed, they braced themselves for the battle ahead, knowing that their struggle for freedom was far from over.

Max's heart raced as the alarm klaxon blared through the corridors of the central control room. The countdown had begun, and with it, a deafening rush of adrenaline and fear engulfed the survivors. The walls shook, and the once sterile air was now thick with the acrid stench of smoke and burning circuits. The central control room, now a war zone, was filled with sparks and the blaring of emergency lights.

Max and his team—Samantha, a former nurse, and Marcus, a mechanic—hurriedly finished wiring the explosives they had managed to salvage from the bunker. The countdown timer on the main screen read 30 minutes. Every second felt like an eternity as they struggled to complete their sabotage.

"Are you sure this will work?" Samantha shouted over the noise, her hands shaking as she secured the final charges.

"It has to," Max replied, his voice strained but resolute. "We don't have any other options. Once this place goes up, the island's infrastructure should collapse. It'll trigger a massive chain reaction."

Marcus, covered in grime and sweat, was furiously typing on a console. "I'm setting up the trigger now. We'll need to get out of here quickly once it's done."

Outside the control room, chaos had taken over the island. The survivors who had chosen to stay behind, led by Alex, had engaged in a final, desperate skirmish with the island's security forces. Drones buzzed overhead, launching tear gas canisters and firebombs. The sky was a swirling mess of black smoke and fire as the island's artificial defenses went into overdrive.

Inside the control room, Max's team worked in frenetic silence, punctuated only by the clattering of tools and the occasional burst of static from a damaged speaker system.

Suddenly, the door to the control room burst open, and a squad of masked soldiers stormed in. Their presence was a stark reminder of the enemies they faced—enemies whose motives remained obscured behind layers of secrecy and manipulation.

"Go! Go!" Max barked. "We need to finish this!"

Samantha and Marcus scrambled to finish their tasks, while Max drew his weapon, ready to defend their position. The soldiers, equipped with high-tech weaponry, began to engage the survivors. The room became a cacophony of gunfire and shouted commands.

Max ducked behind a console, narrowly avoiding a burst of gunfire. He fired back, his bullets finding their mark with deadly precision. Samantha was busy setting up the final charge when a soldier lunged at her. She screamed as she struggled to fend him off, but Marcus managed to shoot the soldier before he could do any more harm.

With the last of the charges in place, Marcus rushed to join Max and Samantha. "It's done! Let's get out of here!"

The team made a hasty retreat through a maintenance tunnel, the walls of which were vibrating with the tremors of the explosions beginning to echo through the island. The tunnel, dimly lit and claustrophobic, seemed to stretch on forever. They could hear the distant roars of the ongoing battle above, and the air was filled with the stench of burning metal and ozone.

As they emerged from the tunnel on the far side of the island, they could see the devastation unfolding. The island's infrastructure was crumbling—buildings collapsing into themselves, fireballs illuminating the sky, and drones falling from the air. The artificial paradise was turning into an apocalyptic wasteland.

Max and his team ran toward the boat dock, their legs burning with exhaustion and fear. They had been so focused on their mission that they hadn't noticed Alex and his faction approaching from the opposite side of the dock.

Alex, now clad in a tactical outfit and carrying a high-powered rifle, appeared with a smirk on his face. "You didn't think you could just walk away, did you?"

Max's eyes widened in shock and anger. "Alex! I should have known you'd be involved in this."

Alex's face was a mask of cold determination. "I've seen what's coming. You're too late. The island's collapse will be a cover for something much bigger. They'll just move us to another location, start the experiment over."

A violent confrontation erupted. Max and Alex exchanged gunfire as their factions clashed in a brutal fight. Samantha and Marcus fought alongside Max, their every move a testament to their desperation and survival instincts.

In the midst of the chaos, Max and Alex engaged in a fierce hand-to-hand combat. Alex's blows were precise and brutal, but Max's training and resolve gave him an edge. The two men grappled, exchanging punches and kicks, neither willing to yield.

At one point, Max managed to land a decisive blow, knocking Alex to the ground. As Max approached, Alex pulled a concealed knife, slashing at Max's side. Max grunted in pain but grabbed Alex's arm, twisting it until the knife clattered away. With one final, determined effort, Max delivered a crushing blow that left Alex incapacitated.

Breathing heavily, Max looked around. The survivors, who had managed to fend off Alex's faction, were regrouping. The dock was now in sight, but the way was strewn with debris and wreckage. The island was collapsing around them, and every second counted.

Max led the survivors to the boat. The vessel, though small and battered, was their only hope of escape. As they boarded, Max checked the engine and fuel levels. Despite the damage, it was operational.

The survivors piled into the boat, their faces etched with exhaustion and relief. Max took the helm, and as the boat slowly moved away from the dock, he glanced back at the burning island. The sight was both a victory and a grim reminder of the horrors they had endured.

As they sailed further from the island, the full scale of their ordeal began to sink in. Max could see the outlines of other islands on the horizon, identical to the one they had just escaped from. The realization was horrifying.

"Look," Samantha said, pointing to the horizon. "Is that... another island?"

Max squinted into the distance, his heart sinking. "It's another one of those islands. We're still trapped in this nightmare."

The survivors were silent, their faces reflecting the gravity of their situation. The experiment had not ended; it had merely evolved. The world they had known was a facade, and the island had been a mere piece of a much larger, more sinister puzzle.

Max's thoughts raced as he tried to process the implications. They had escaped one hell, only to find themselves on the brink of another. The shadows of the experiment loomed large, casting a dark cloud over their newfound freedom.

In the dim light of the boat, Max could see the survivors' faces—some hopeful, some resigned. They had survived the island, but the true extent of their predicament was only beginning to unfold. The horizon promised no solace, only the continuation of their harrowing journey.

Chapter 12: The Terrifying Truth

The oppressive heat of the island had reached its peak as Max, Jodie, and the few remaining survivors stumbled down the crumbling path toward the far side of the island. The air was thick with a tension that seemed almost palpable, as if the very atmosphere was holding its breath in anticipation of what was to come. The island was a war zone now, its once lush and serene landscape torn apart by the chaos unleashed by the self-destruct sequence.

Max's heart raced as he led the way, his mind racing even faster. The countdown clock on the central control room had shown only minutes remaining when they had fled. Their only hope now was the boat they had spotted in the distance—a small, unassuming vessel that seemed to promise freedom and a return to civilization. But Max couldn't shake the nagging feeling that their ordeal might not be over.

As they approached the dock, the boat came into clearer view. It was a modest craft, with a single outboard motor and just enough room for them to escape. Jodie, her face streaked with dirt and sweat, was already aboard, checking the vessel's condition. The others, their faces showing a mix of exhaustion and hope, followed closely behind.

"Is it seaworthy?" Max asked, panting heavily.

Jodie looked up from her inspection, nodding. "It looks like it. The engine's functional, and there's enough fuel to get us out of here."

Max's gaze swept over the group. They were a ragtag assembly of survivors—some of whom had seen their friends and family perish, others who had been twisted by the psychological manipulation of the island. Despite their differences, they had forged a tenuous bond in their shared suffering.

"Alright," Max said, trying to steady his voice. "Let's get out of here. We need to put as much distance between ourselves and this place as possible."

The survivors clambered onto the boat, and Jodie took the helm. Max, his hands still trembling from the adrenaline, watched as she started the engine. The boat sputtered to life, and the low hum of the motor cut through the eerie silence of the island.

As they drifted away from the dock, the island began to recede into the distance. Max's eyes stayed fixed on the horizon, his mind racing through the events of the past weeks. They had survived unimaginable horrors, confronted their deepest fears, and discovered the dark truth behind the island's true purpose. Yet, as they left the island behind, a sense of foreboding still lingered.

Max turned to Jodie, who was concentrating on navigating through the choppy waters. "Do you have any idea where we're heading?" he asked.

Jodie shook her head. "I'm not sure. We'll have to rely on the boat's navigation equipment. Hopefully, we'll find a shipping lane or a nearby island."

Max nodded, trying to keep his worries at bay. The boat moved steadily through the water, leaving the ruined island behind. The survivors huddled together, their faces illuminated by the pale light of the setting sun.

Hours passed, and the sun dipped below the horizon, casting a golden glow over the ocean. The survivors tried to find comfort in the fading light, but the weight of their experiences hung heavy over them. They had faced death, betrayal, and psychological torment, and now they were left to confront the uncertainty of what lay ahead.

As night fell, Max took a seat next to the boat's navigation console. He examined the charts and instruments, hoping to get a better understanding of their position. His fingers traced the lines on the map, searching for any signs of nearby land.

Suddenly, Jodie called out from the helm. "Max, come here! You need to see this."

Max rushed over, his heart pounding. Jodie pointed to the horizon, where a faint, almost imperceptible glow was visible. Max squinted, trying to make out what it was.

"It looks like another island," Jodie said, her voice tinged with concern.

Max's heart sank. "Another island? Are you sure?"

Jodie nodded. "It's too far to be anything else. We need to check it out."

Max nodded, his mind racing. If there was another island in the distance, it could mean that their ordeal was far from over. He turned to the survivors, who were gathered around, their expressions a mix of exhaustion and curiosity.

"We're heading toward that glow," Max said. "It might be our only chance to find out if we're truly free or if this nightmare is far from over."

The boat changed course, heading toward the distant glow. The survivors fell silent, their faces illuminated by the dim light of the boat's navigation lights. The journey felt interminable, each passing minute stretching into what felt like an eternity.

As they approached the glowing island, the lights of the boat began to reveal more details. The outline of the island became clearer, and Max's heart dropped as he saw the familiar features of the landscape. It was unmistakable—the island they had left behind, identical in every way.

The boat slowed as it neared the shore. Max and the others stared in disbelief as they realized the horrifying truth. They had not escaped. They had only been led to another island that was part of the same experiment.

Max's mind raced as he grappled with the implications. The island they had left was not an isolated experiment—it was just one of many. The revelation that they had not truly escaped sent a wave of despair through the survivors.

Jodie's voice broke the silence. "What do we do now?"

Max looked around at the faces of the survivors. They had fought so hard to escape, only to find themselves back at the beginning. The sense of betrayal was almost palpable.

"We need to figure out how to get off this island," Max said, his voice resolute. "We can't give up. There has to be a way out."

The survivors nodded, their determination reignited by Max's words. They had faced unimaginable challenges and survived against all odds. Now, they had to confront the ultimate betrayal and find a way to escape the clutches of the experiment.

As they prepared to explore the new island, Max's thoughts turned to the documents they had found on the boat. They had hinted at a larger conspiracy, a network of islands designed to test and manipulate. If they were to survive, they would need to uncover the full extent of the experiment and find a way to break free.

The survivors disembarked from the boat, their faces etched with a mixture of fear and determination. They were stepping into the unknown, but they had no choice but to press on. The nightmare of the island was far from over, and their fight for survival was only beginning.

Max took a deep breath and led the way into the darkness of the new island. The journey ahead was uncertain, but he was determined to uncover the truth and find a way to escape the clutches of the hostile horizon.

The boat rocked gently beneath their feet as they cut through the dark waters, the island shrinking into the distance. Silence had settled over the survivors, broken only by the hum of the boat's motor. Max stood at the bow, his mind racing. It should've felt like victory—like freedom—but a knot of dread twisted in his gut. He clutched the folder he'd taken from the facility, its contents still sealed within.

Ethan, bloodied and bruised but alive, sat beside Talia, who stared blankly ahead, her eyes hollow after losing too many people along the way. They'd all lost too much. Behind them, the island—once a place of mysterious beauty—now looked like a smudge on the horizon, barely visible in the early morning light.

Max hesitated, his hands shaking as he finally tore open the folder. The documents were thin, almost as if their contents were purposefully minimal, but what was there was more than enough to send a chill down his spine. Schematics of other islands, encrypted data logs, and a series of names—hundreds of them. He scanned the papers, his heart pounding as he saw not just the names of the survivors, but the names of people from all over the world. Test subjects. His hand froze when he saw his own name printed neatly on the first page.

"How long until we're out of range?" Ethan's voice was strained, still weak from the injuries he'd sustained during the final assault.

Max didn't answer. He couldn't. His eyes were glued to a small map tucked into the back of the file, its lines drawn meticulously, a chain of islands forming a ring far larger than the one they'd escaped from. It wasn't just one experiment. It never had been. The implications hit him like a sledgehammer, making his knees weak.

"Max?" Talia's voice was soft, uncertain.

He turned to her, meeting her eyes. She'd seen too much—too much death, too much betrayal. They all had. But this... this was worse. He handed her the documents, his voice thick with disbelief. "It's not over."

She frowned as she skimmed the pages, her expression shifting from confusion to shock to horror. "No... no, this can't be right." She passed the papers to Ethan, her hand trembling. "Tell me this isn't real."

Ethan, his face already pale from blood loss, looked like a ghost as he read the contents. "We... we were never supposed to make it out," he whispered.

Max's gaze drifted to the horizon, where a sliver of land began to come into view. At first, it seemed like a mirage, a trick of the light after the days of chaos and bloodshed. But it was no illusion. The shape of the island was unmistakable—tall cliffs rising sharply from the sea, a dense jungle beyond, and the familiar hum of technology lurking beneath its surface. It was a mirror image of the hell they'd just escaped from.

"No..." Talia's voice was barely audible, her hands clutching the edge of the boat as if she could will it to turn around. "We got out. We're free. This can't be happening."

Max felt the cold grip of hopelessness wrap around his heart. They hadn't escaped. They were still trapped in the experiment, pawns in a game that stretched far beyond the single island. And now, as they approached the next island, the terrifying realization dawned on him. The experiment wasn't confined to just one place, one location. It was endless.

"They're watching us," Max muttered, the truth sinking in. "They've always been watching us."

Ethan staggered to his feet, his face contorted with fury. "No, this ends now! We can't just... we can't just keep running in circles like lab rats. We need to fight back!"

"How?" Talia asked, her voice breaking. "We barely made it off the last island. We lost so many people—"

"We didn't escape," Max interrupted, his voice colder than he intended. "We were let go. They wanted us to think we had a chance, but it was all part of the game."

Talia's eyes filled with tears, her fists clenching at her sides. "So what are we supposed to do? Just let them win? Let them keep controlling us?"

Max stared at the approaching island, the sinking dread in his stomach becoming unbearable. He knew the answer. They couldn't fight back. Not like this. Not without knowing the full scope of the experiment. But they could still survive. They had to. Maybe there was a way to outsmart whoever was behind this nightmare. Maybe there was still hope.

But as the boat drew closer to the island, his resolve began to falter. The drone of unseen machines buzzed in the distance, faint but unmistakable. It was the same sound they had heard on the first island—the sound of their captors, always watching, always waiting.

"There's no turning back," Max said quietly, more to himself than to the others.

Ethan slammed his fist against the side of the boat, the metallic clang echoing across the water. "Damn it! We can't just keep doing this, Max. We can't keep playing their game."

Max didn't respond. He knew Ethan was right. But the question remained—what choice did they have? Even if they tried to escape again, who was to say they wouldn't just end up on another island, another iteration of the same twisted experiment?

Talia wiped her eyes, her voice shaky but determined. "Maybe... maybe there's something different about this island. Maybe we can find answers here. Find a way to stop it."

Max glanced at her, seeing the desperation in her eyes. He wanted to believe her. He wanted to believe there was still a chance to end this nightmare. But every instinct told him that this was just the beginning of another round, another layer of manipulation.

The boat slowed as they approached the shoreline. Max stood at the front, scanning the beach for any signs of movement, but it was eerily quiet. Too quiet. The jungle loomed in the distance, dense and impenetrable, just like the last island. He could feel the eyes of their captors on them, even if he couldn't see them.

"We need a plan," Max said, his voice steady despite the chaos in his mind. "We can't just walk into this blindly. If this island is anything like the last one, it's full of traps, surveillance, and God knows what else."

Ethan nodded, though his anger still simmered beneath the surface. "Right. We stick together this time. No more splitting up. We scout the area, find shelter, and figure out what the hell is going on."

Max glanced at Talia, who was already checking their supplies. She looked exhausted, both physically and emotionally, but there was still a fire in her eyes. She wasn't ready to give up, not yet.

As they prepared to disembark, Max's gaze returned to the distant horizon. For a brief moment, he imagined what might be beyond these islands—if there was a real world out there, untouched by the experiment. He couldn't shake the feeling that the world they once knew was long gone, if it had ever existed at all.

Stepping onto the soft sand, Max's mind was already racing through possibilities. The island might hold the answers they needed, or it might be another layer of deception. But one thing was certain: they couldn't afford to trust anyone—not even each other.

They moved cautiously, the weight of their situation pressing down on them with every step. The jungle was silent, save for the occasional rustle of leaves in the breeze. But Max knew better. He could feel the invisible eyes watching their every move, waiting for them to make a mistake.

Talia paused, her hand resting on Max's arm. "Do you think... do you think anyone's survived this before?"

Max didn't answer immediately. He didn't want to admit the truth—not to her, not to Ethan, not even to himself. But deep down, he knew the odds were against them. Whatever this experiment was, it wasn't designed for them to survive.

As they ventured deeper into the jungle, the shadows seemed to close in around them. Every step felt like a step closer to the edge of a precipice, and Max couldn't shake the feeling that they were walking into another trap.

But this time, they wouldn't go down without a fight.

Because even if the experiment never ended, even if the world beyond was a lie, they still had one thing their captors didn't expect.

Each other.

And that, Max hoped, might be enough.

Don't miss out!

Visit the website below and you can sign up to receive emails whenever Michael Ferguson publishes a new book. There's no charge and no obligation.

https://books2read.com/r/B-A-CKNW-RCVZE

BOOKS 2 READ

Connecting independent readers to independent writers.

Did you love *Hostile Horizon*? Then you should read *Shattered Crown*[1] by Michael Ferguson!

[2]

In the war-torn empire of Rethnor, the gods have been silent for centuries, and their once-mighty temples lie in ruins. Rival kingdoms vie for control, while an ancient, unspeakable evil stirs beneath the surface, threatening to plunge the world into eternal darkness.

Kade, a disgraced warrior-priest known as the Holy Blade, lives in exile after betraying the very gods he once served. Haunted by guilt and visions of the gods' fall, he is offered a chance at redemption: recover the legendary Crown of the

---

1. https://books2read.com/u/4AMQ0q

2. https://books2read.com/u/4AMQ0q

Fallen, a powerful relic said to have the ability to resurrect the gods and restore balance to the world.

But Kade knows a terrible secret—he was complicit in the gods' downfall, and their destruction was not what it seemed. As he embarks on his dangerous quest, a ragtag group of outcasts and misfits joins him: Mira, a powerful mage with a hidden past; Tyra, a young thief who claims to have seen the gods in her dreams; and Sorin, a mercenary with questionable loyalties. Together, they navigate treacherous lands, from desolate wastelands to haunted forests, seeking the Crown's true location.

As the group draws closer to their goal, Kade's darkest secret begins to unravel. His bloodline is bound to the ancient evil—the very force the gods sacrificed themselves to contain. The Crown, far from being a tool for salvation, is revealed to be the key to unleashing this malevolent entity upon the world. And the only way to stop it is for Kade to make the ultimate sacrifice: his own daughter, Lyra, who was thought lost long ago, but is now revealed to be the vessel for the ancient evil.

Caught between love and duty, redemption and damnation, Kade must decide whether to save the world by destroying everything he holds dear or release the evil that could end all life. As alliances fracture and dark forces close in, Kade and his companions face an impossible choice: will they fight for a future built on sacrifice, or will they surrender to the forces of darkness?

In Shattered Crown, the fate of the world lies in the hands of a man whose very bloodline is cursed, a group of misfits bound by fragile trust, and a relic that could either save or doom them all. This epic fantasy blends intense action, moral complexity, and world-shattering stakes into a tale that will leave readers breathless. As Kade's journey unfolds, nothing is as it seems, and the ultimate question remains—can redemption truly be found, or are some sins unforgivable?

www.ingramcontent.com/pod-product-compliance
Lightning Source LLC
Chambersburg PA
CBHW071318130726
47996CB00002B/525